Curious Tales for Curious Folk

Edited by
Callum Pearce

First Edition Published By
House Of Loki
Professor Teldersstraat 372
Vlaardingen, Nederland 3132AZ
KVK : 93090900
This is a work of fiction. Similarities to real people,
places, or events are entirely coincidental.
Curious Tales For Curious Folk
ISBN: **978-90-835-3953-9**
Cover Design and Concept by Greenspike
www.greenspike-art.com
Formatted by Callum Pearce
Edited by Callum Pearce

Copyright © 2025 House Of Loki

Contents

THE FARM
   By Karen B. Jones.................................
9
BIRD TAILS AND BIRD TALES
   by Trent Redfield.................................
17
SURVIVING A NIGHT ALONE IN THE DARK
   By Gary Rubidge...................................
29
BAMBOOZLED
   By Lisa H Owens...................................
49
MEMORIAE
   By Jonathan J Bowerman......................
65
FROM THE STARS
   By Emil Haskett....................................
83
THE SNAGGLETOOTH WUUF
   By Tom Folske......................................
93

A DEAL WITH THE DEVIL
   By Brian MacGowan 107

DON'T CROSS MOTHER
   By Lady Lyndsey Holloway 125

THE LEGEND OF TOM MCCOY
   By Dawn DeBraal 159

THE PARROT MAN
   By John Clewarth 173

CURIOUS CUTHBERT
   By Lynne Phillips 195

HORROR HIGH SCHOOL FOREVER
   By Destiny Eve Pifer 213

MEET THE AUTHORS 221

THE FARM
By Karen B. Jones

It's October. The time of the year when days grew shorter and shadows deepened. Growing up, I had always been afraid of the dark. Unseen things scratched at second-floor windows, imaginary knocks on doors that didn't exist, and whispers drifting down from the sealed attic space above my head. The one constant in our lives had always been the pumpkin patch.

"Johnnie, go weed the pumpkins. Take care not to disturb them," Dad would say, a glazed look on his face.

"But, Dad! There aren't any weeds. Besides, there's something wrong with those pumpkins. Can't you feel it?"

"Do as you're told, Johnnie," my father sighed. "They're just pumpkins."

When my parents died, they left me the farm. Their last will and testament made one thing clear. It was mine to do with as I chose, but the pumpkin patch had to be left undisturbed; it had to be.

You know pumpkins? Big orange things that my mother never made anything with. Usually, pumpkins died back and needed replanting each year. Not ours! As far back as I could remember, our patch came back every year by itself. One old-timer told us that our pumpkins had "naturalised."

"Hogwash!" Dad scoffed. "Pumpkins don't naturalise. They're annuals, not perennials."

Regardless, they returned like clockwork. Nothing else would grow in the ground where they've been, either. Trust me when I say we tried.

"Cursed land," the old-timer retorted to Dad's retreating backside. "Witches' land! Don't you dare eat those pumpkins! Cursed, they are!"

As an impressionable, scared-of-the-dark boy of 8, his words terrified me. It would be many years before I understood.

***

The root cellar always had a lock on it. Now, by myself, I saw no need to keep it that way. Unable to find the key, I took a sledgehammer to it, hitting the lock repeatedly until the hasp broke. Staring at the hundreds of jars stored in the root cellar—all filled with pumpkin—I noticed each had a faded date marked on its face. The oldest were unreadable; however, I could barely make out a few dates, the oldest still legible with a 1692 scratched into the glass. Since they appeared in date order, it stood to reason there were some much, much older. Looking at them, I had just convinced myself they were talking to me and glowing when everything went black.

The sun had risen when I awoke. I hadn't the foggiest idea how I wound up in bed. Standing in the root cellar, staring at those accursed jars, was the last thing I remembered. Nightmares had plagued my sleep: floating headstones and screaming, disembodied wisps rising from the pumpkin patch cloaked in fog, jars of pumpkin talking to me. For all that, I was grateful. For the first time in recent memory, the morning sun broke through the grime on the windows, filling the room with welcome respite from the darkness and shadows. Besides, it was just nightmares. Right?

***

My parents' absence left a hole in my heart. After Mom and Dad went to their great rewards—just weeks apart—I needed something to occupy my thoughts and time.

I turned their upstairs bedroom into a library. Bookshelves covered the walls from floor to ceiling, window to window. I saw no need for a door since there was just me, so I made it into a makeshift desk, doorknob, and all. I know it sounds impressive, but it wasn't—scrap lumber from the barn for shelves and a rickety ladder-back chair held together with rusty nails from the attic. My last chore was to turn the window facing the pumpkin patch into a window seat—a place I could sit watching in relative comfort. Impressive, and maybe just a bit weird, were the books.

When I travelled, which I managed to do more often since it was just me, my piddling inheritance went to buying books. Everything I could find on witchcraft, magic, and Halloween. Who knew there would be so much available? I could have quickly filled two rooms with the treasures I had found. So, when the shelves filled, I stacked my many finds on the floor. It's not hoarding if it's books, right?

The farm fell into ever-declining levels of disarray; it wasn't my priority. The pumpkin patch that kept coming back year after year, however, was. Spending all my time reading, that damnable piece of earth became my only obsession, and the closer Halloween came, the more manic my desire to get answers. Books sat propped open throughout the house, each page about possession marked with a sliver of paper.

Sleepless nights filled with screaming pumpkins and full-bodied, floating apparitions took their toll. There was only one week left until Halloween, and I had wasted days sitting at the upstairs bedroom window watching the patch. It wasn't like I was sleeping, anyway.

Ghostly apparitions of the long-dead, maniacal laughing pumpkins with snarling grins and living scarecrows plagued not just my nights but also my days. The whispers from my childhood were back, only now I understood what they were saying.

"Just break them. You know you want to. Destroy the source of all your fears. You know you'll feel better if you do."

The disembodied chattering went on night after night. Drawn and worn, my skin sagging and sallow, what had started all those years ago as bad dreams had turned the farm into a living nightmare.

On Halloween Eve, convinced by the whispers that the jars were indeed the source of all that was wrong with the farm, I took Dad's axe, marched to the root cellar, and broke every last jar.

They came flooding out in waves—the souls of hundreds of witches. Held at bay by something as simple as enchanted pumpkins and glass jars, they poured out of the root cellar and into the night. It was midnight—Halloween had arrived.

What had I done? Dropping to my knees, I covered

both my ears, trying to block out the screams. I couldn't tell if they were theirs or mine. Something dark and evil marched into the spongy recesses of my brain, demanding I pay attention. I should have been afraid. I should have taken it as a warning. I did neither.

One particularly warty ghost witch with rotting teeth and horrible breath floated inches from my upturned face.

"Thank you, Johnnie. It took us years to convince you to destroy our prison. Now, we are free!

Wait! What is this? What is this?!?"

They were beyond angry. Shrieks of joy turned into howls of disbelief. The spell placed on the farm by a druid priest bent on ridding the world of witches hundreds of years before held firm. The witches had nowhere to escape to, remaining trapped on the Farm. Where I failed, the unknown druid succeeded. I felt vindicated, at least for a second.

"As payment for the disservice you have inflicted on us, you will become one of us," the old hag screamed at me, foul spittle splattering my cheeks.

And, just like that, I became what I had feared my entire life—something that went bump, scratched, and clawed in the night.

The Farm wasn't just a farm; the pumpkin patch was not a simple patch, and every owner became a prison guard, unbeknownst to them. The old timer had been right all along. The jars, meticulously filled with possessed pumpkin parts, were beyond repair; that was on me.

There would always be new farm owners. They cleaned out the root cellar and started canning pumpkins again, oblivious to the reason, just going about the task. More of the spell woven into the fabric of the farm?

When the field grew four times as big the following fall, the witches found themselves back in their pumpkin prisons, me included. Staring through the hollow eye sockets of my pumpkin prison, I watched as the new owners burned my beloved books into piles of ash. The "devil's work", they called it. Of course, at "harvest time," I was the first to go under the knife.

The root cellar, locked once again, was dark. Nailed shut using boards from my bookshelves, even the tiny window that let in barely any light was no more. The dark I feared was back with a vengeance. However, the witches had stopped their incessant prattling.

I guess in everything bad, if you look hard enough, you might find a silver lining. Or, in this case, an orange one. Sighing, I resigned myself to my fate. My nightmare was complete. **THE END**

BIRD TAILS AND BIRD TALES
By Trent Redfield

Awakened by singing starlings, Captain Matteo Gallo opened his eyes.

Pain.

Sharp, agonising pain flooded his senses. He bit down hard, teeth clenched and grinding, pushing back against the smothering unconsciousness that threatened to take him under.

Matteo dug his fingers into the dirt, gripping the earth to steady himself. Once again, he bit down hard. His teeth cut the inside of his cheek, and he tasted blood. He concentrated on the pain and taste. By focusing on it, he maintained his grip on the waking world and was able to focus on what was happening around him.

He heard the singing birds. He switched his concentration to the bird calls that were echoing throughout the forested landscape. Those calls had awakened him. They might even help keep him awake.

"Where am I? What happened?" he muttered. Hearing his own words centred him and as he tried to sort through his most recent memories, his mind moved further away from the shadows that might have taken him away forever. He needed to stay awake and focused or he would be lost. He had to stay iconcious.

He remembered being in a fight. "Those damned Deirda! Those shape-changing witches! They tricked me with their hedge magic! I should have known better," his voice was a mix of anger, resentment, embarrassment, and regret.

"Those three kids pushed me off the hill. One could turn into a bird, another into a wolf, and their leader became a cat. Together, as animals, they overcame me. It was the one that changes into a damned cat that sliced the ropes holding the cut logs, crashing them down onto me!"

Matteo started to look around. He searched the ground near him with his hands. He looked around. He listened carefully. Were the Deirda gone? Or were those bird noises one of them?

He lifted his hands away from the dirt and found himself partially buried in soil, rocks, and cut timber. "The damned Deirda sent a landslide down on me! I am lucky to even be alive." He pushed slowly and carefully against the logs, letting them roll and tumble away from him.

Everything hurt.

Everything.

Captain Matteo Gallo was a member of the Tyrsus Empire's military. He had trained at the capital's military academy. He was serving at the frontline in the war against the Deirda.

As a soldier, he knew wounds and injuries. His were serious. His legs and arms were bruised and battered. He certainly had a concussion. It hurt to breathe. That meant broken ribs.

Matteo pushed himself to one knee.

His body screamed in pain and agony.

He forced himself to slowly stand up.

He wanted to lie back down and sleep, but he knew if he did, he would never awaken. Matteo stepped away from the pile of logs, dirt, and rocks that could easily have become his grave. He saw his shattered crossbow in the rubble. Though his scabbard was still somehow attached to his belt, his sword was missing, and so was his shield.

None of his soldiers were close by, nor were any of the loggers who had been hired to cut the timber for a planned Tyrsus Empire fort. Above him rose a hill that had once been domed, but the dome had cracked and split away a long time ago. The split dome had created a shelf of rock and it was there that the Deirda girl, in the shape of a lynx, had clawed the ropes and sent the crashing logs down upon him. She was gone, and so were her two companions. He was alone. The birds calling and singing around him were just wild birds, the only creatures he could see or hear.

Matteo was hit by a wave of dizziness and nausea. Standing took so much had taken so much of his energy and concentration.

His vision lost focus. The strange, broken, domed hill blurred. He thought for a moment he saw it intact and whole. He saw the rounded tor as it must have been in ages past. He imagined music, singing, and voices in the woods around him. Starlings and other songbirds called and sang in time with the unseen musicians.

He crumpled to one knee, but shaking his head helped force away the vision, and the strange hallucination ended.

"The concussion must be worse than I thought," he whispered as he stood again, more slowly and carefully than before. "I must have taken a serious blow to the head. I do not even recognise the language of the song in the vision."

"What song? What am I thinking? That was all imagined. I need to move away from here. It is getting darker." He found that if he spoke aloud, it focused and centred him. He turned toward the direction he knew the Tyrsus forces were camped and concentrated on putting one foot in front of the other.

Slowed by his injuries and taking care not to overexert himself, Matteo's pace was slow. He looked for the easiest paths, picking out animal trails to ease his passage. As he walked, darkness crept in and twilight descended. He did not know how long he had been lying unconscious.

He needed to keep walking for as long as he could and find his camp. He needed to focus. He listened to the birds and used their song as a way to anchor himself to reality and focus on walking toward his goal.

As he walked, he found himself singing softly. Captain Mateo Gallo, warrior and hardened soldier, did not sing. The enlisted men drank and sang, but Captain Mateo Gallo was a product of the Tyrsus Military Academy. He was disciplined and proud.

"What am I doing? Singing? And what is the song?" As his words left his mouth, he knew what he was singing. It was the song from the vision. In a language he did not recognise. The song that the birds had echoed in the hallucination. He stopped, confused and bewildered. The forest was dense and dark around him.

From amongst the trees, his singing was echoed back to him. The song bounced through the forest. He did not know where the source was, but it was nearby.

The language was again unknown to him, it was the song he had been singing, but in a soft, melodious tone. It was not birdsong, but after the unknown singer stopped, the starlings mimicked the mysterious tune.

Matteo immediately stopped. He grabbed a stout branch from the forest floor. His hand missed the leather grip of his sword handle and he wished he had a shield, but he would have to make do with his makeshift club. When he moved into a fighting stance, quiet descended over the forest. The singing and every other sound disappeared.

Was the singing just more hallucination? He knew his injuries could cause his mind to reel and his senses to be clouded. He had seen it in many soldiers, especially from falls and other head injuries. He gripped his club and stepped forward.

The darkness increased. Was he even going the right way? The broken domed hill, the only landmark he would recognise, was long gone from view, but he thought he was headed toward the military encampment of the Tyrsus Empire.

"Hello to you and hello from me. Where do you hail from? Where do you head to? Our paths cross and our fates entwine. Hello to you and hello from me," sang someone from the darkness behind Matteo.

It was a clear, strong song. There was no way he was

imagining it. He turned to look down the path.

There was a creature standing on the pathway. It was pale-skinned, with long white hair tied in a ponytail, high cheekbones, a slim build, athletic, and fit. They wore a loose linen shirt, leather pants, and leather boots. The clothes were well-made, but in a style from at least a generation ago. They were not of the Tyrsus Empire, and Matteo did not believe he was looking at one of the Deirda either. This person, or creature, was something else entirely.

"Hello to you and hello from me. Where do you hail from? Where do you head to? Our paths cross and our fates entwine. Hello to you and hello from me," came the song again. This pale creature, beautiful and mysterious, was singing to Matteo.

"Who are you? What are you?" Matteo yelled as he raised his club. "Step any closer and you will regret it. I will smash in that pretty white head!"

"Hello to you and hello from me. You are lost. I have found you. I am wild. I am forest-bound and forest-kin. I offer no harm except to any who threaten the forest, forest-kin, and chosen of the fey-kind. Hello to you and hello from me," the creature answered in song.

"Hello to you and hello from me. Hello to you and hello from me. Hello to you and hello from me," echoed a flock of starlings that Matteo had not previously seen in the trees. The air was filled with their perfect mimicry of the creature's song.

Matteo spun around to look at the gathered birds, bewildered and frightened by their sudden appearance. As he looked back down the path, the creature was gone. Matteo crept slowly and deliberately to where the creature had been. He saw no footprints or any other indication of it having been there or where it might have gone.

"I offer no harm except to any that threaten forest, forest-kin, and chosen of the fey-kind," sang the starlings from the branches above Matteo. He turned and walked away as quickly as his injuries allowed.

"I need to leave. I need to find Tyrsus forces. We will burn this forest and any strange creatures we find within! Then we will hunt down and kill the Deirda! I will kill those three shape-changing kids myself!" he growled as he pushed his way down the forest path. The trees were thicker here. The pathway narrowed. Matteo could see he was approaching a T-intersection.

"The right path will be the right path," he chuckled, "See, I can play with words as well as you," he shouted out to the dark forest.

"Hello to you and hello from me," spoke the creature who was now standing at the T-intersection. "I offer no harm except to any that threaten forest, forest-kin, and chosen of the fey-kind. Axe and flame harm fey, forest, and friend. Hello to you and hello from me."

"I do not know what you are, but you are in my way. I am going down this path, and you cannot stop me," Matteo raised his club and stalked toward the pale creature.

The creature smiled. Perfect white teeth, sharp and pointed, were visible to Matteo as the creature's cold grin greeted him. The creature raised a hand, "Hello to you and hello from me. You are no friend to the forest and the forest is no friend to thee. Hello to you and hello from me." The creature snapped his fingers.

Matteo heard a sudden hiss close by. His club had changed into a serpent! Before he could react, the snake sank fangs deep into his hand. Matteo screamed, dropping the slithering snake.

"You are no friend to the forest and the forest is no friend to thee," sang the starlings as laughter rang from the creature's mouth. The creature spoke, "Hello to you and hello from me. I offer no harm except to any who threaten forest, forest-kin, and chosen of the fey-kind. Axe and flame harm fey, forest, and friend. You are no friend to the forest and the forest is no friend to thee. Hello to you and hello from me."

Matteo's bitten hand was swelling and blackening. He now knew the snake was venomous, but he had not recognised the species. He looked down to see if he could figure out what kind of serpent had bitten him, but at his feet lay the club and no snake was visible.

"What are you? What have you done to me?" Matteo shouted at the creature. Matteo was no longer trying to hide his fear. He was shaking. The snake venom, the presence of this strange creature, and his injuries were catching up with him.

"Hello to you and hello from me. I am fairy-folk, faerie-kind, and forest fey. I am the guardian of the forest, forest folk, and forest friends. You are no friend to the forest and the forest is no friend to thee. You hunt the forest friends, the Deirda-folk. I guardian. I protector. We will break your axes. We will extinguish your fires. We will shatter your swords. Hello to you and hello from me," the creature spoke while opening his mouth into an impossibly wide smile, showing those sharp teeth and gazing at Matteo with malice.

"We will break your axes. We will extinguish your fires. We will shatter your swords," sang the starlings. More birds joined them. Ravens and crows called out the menacing words as well, filling the forest with a cacophony of threats.

Matteo's hand was growing black. The venom was spreading. He was sweating. His breath was becoming more shallow.

He gazed at the creature. The creature still smiled and raised both his hands, gesturing at Matteo and clapped his hands together three times.

Awakened by singing starlings, Captain Matteo Gallo opened his eyes.

Pain.

Sharp, agonising pain flooded his senses. He bit down hard, teeth clenched and grinding, pushing back against the smothering unconsciousness that threatened to take him under.

Matteo dug his fingers into the dirt, gripping onto the earth to steady himself. As he clawed at the ground, pain shot through his hand. Matteo looked and saw that the hand was swollen and black. In the flesh were two fang marks oozing yellow pus.

THE END

SURVIVING A NIGHT ALONE IN THE DARK
By Gary Rubidge

Good morning, class. Our assignment was to write a scary story. Well, when I think about it, there's not much that scares me now. I've decided to share my actual experience instead of writing a crummy story like everyone else is writing. It happened not long ago when a lot of weird stuff happened, and I met some interesting characters.

Imagine this.

I thought we were old enough and smart enough by now to know what to do when we find ourselves in a scary situation, thanks to the shows on TV and movies in the cinemas that have shown us what we should and shouldn't do. Even many of the games online show you how best to handle these situations. However, it seems most people are prime candidates for Darwin's Theory of Evolution (Survival of the Fittest) if their stories are to be believed. The scary movies always show the lady deciding that Nighttime during a storm is a good time to have a shower. People wander around in their underwear, then go outside in the dark with a candle, calling out "who's there?" The guys always bravely wander into the dark to investigate the noise. Guess what? They all die horrible deaths!

Zombies aren't scary! Watch shows like 'The Walking Dead'. The characters get a virus, like COVID or something, and spread it by biting you. Sure, they have grey skin hanging off their faces. Big, yellow, unblinking eyes and long, sharp teeth. They stomp around on straight legs with their arms out in front, making horrible, squelchy noises. People scream when they see them, but don't run away. Then they die and become zombies themselves. I tell you now, there's no way I'd be paralysed to the spot. It's easy enough to run, so why don't they run? I'll tell you why. It's because you can't make a movie or TV show if everyone did what they should.

Vampires like Dracula can't touch us, bite our necks and suck our blood if we're wearing a cross like I do, or hang garlic around our necks. If we keep them busy until Dawn, then they must go away or turn to dust.

Ghosts can't touch us. They pass through everything as they drift around old buildings and make things go 'bump' in the night! It's hard to hurt someone if you can't touch them!

Go ahead. Look it up online. Every site will tell you

what to do when confronted by one of these creatures. You may as well because you spend most of your life looking online anyway.

What about if you're trapped and can't get away? What if it really is a matter of life and death? What if these scary things are as scared of us as we are of them? What if this fear never leaves? – even after it should've? What if you are the only one who can see it? And what if you are the only one it is after? This is my story. It's what happened to me during those storms late last year. Honest.

A huge storm was already blowing when I went to bed. Lightning turned night into day. Howling winds rattled the windows, causing loose boards to bang. You know the sort of noises a ghost makes? That was the noise the wind made in the house that night. I couldn't sleep.

Mum's a nurse and knew what to give me to help me get to sleep. Dad's a cop. He protected me by leaving a light on and checking everywhere in the bedroom to make me feel safe. He even looked under the bed, because we all know that's where the horrible, scary creatures hide.

I was fast asleep when "Boom!"

I nearly fell out of bed.

I like lightning. It lights up the room when it flashes

across the sky.

I hate thunder!

Peering out from under the covers, I saw the bedroom and hall lights had been turned off, and it was completely dark. I'm talking so dark you could barely see your own hand when it's in front of your face. My heart raced so fast I thought it would burst right out of my chest. I chose to run to mum and dad's room instead of calling out. They'd know what to do.

Luckily, I remembered the monsters under my bed. Would they still be lurking in the dark, waiting to grab me and drag me screaming under the bed with them, never to be seen again? Or would they have crawled out from under the bed and be waiting in the darkest corners of my room? Either way, the thought of large claws, protruding fangs dripping with saliva and sharp teeth that can cut you in two doesn't appeal to me. You may laugh, but that's what I reckon these monsters looked like.

I could hear them.

I called out for Mum and Dad.

Nobody came.

I needed to go to the toilet, so I slowly climbed out of the covers, careful not to make any noise.

But the bed springs squeaked.

The light switch was on the wall next to the door.

I knew that if I turned the light on, then the monsters couldn't get me. You see, everyone knows monsters fear the light, right?

A flash of lightning lit up the room for the briefest moment, allowing me to see that the door was closed. I jumped off the bed, sprinted to the bedroom door and switched on the light.

It wasn't working.

I opened the door and ran to Mum and Dad's bedroom, calling out as I ran. I really hoped the monsters didn't chase me.

Mum and Dad weren't in bed.

I was lucky that the monsters hadn't come after me. They must've been waiting for me to come back to the room so they could get me and do horrible things. I don't need to explain what they could do. We all have a vivid imagination. Just think of the most horrible thing that can happen to you and that's what a monster could do. Well, that wasn't going to happen to me because I was going downstairs to find something to protect myself with. No way I was gonna be killed with nothing on like those stupid women on TV.

First, I needed to go to the toilet. I put on my dad's dressing gown to make myself look bigger, then I went to the toilet in the bathroom next to their bedroom. I couldn't have held on much longer. I kept the toilet door open to see if anything was creeping into the room. The rain was pouring down in sheets against the bedroom window. When the lightning flashed across the sky, all I could see was water spattering against the window.

Dad always makes sure we have torches in the house for times like this. He kept them in his wardrobe. If they were there, I couldn't find them. Bugger!

I took some deep breaths, then slowly let my breath out to calm down, just the way Dad taught me, then crept slowly down the stairs so as not to make any noise in the dark. My back hugged the wall all the way to the kitchen. I was thirsty. My mouth felt like a desert. My eyes were wide, like saucers. They'd become used to the dark, but I still felt my heart pounding in my chest. It seemed to be so loud, I was sure the monsters would hear it.

None of the lights were working. Everything remained dark.

Shadows danced across the table and chairs as lightning streaked across the sky. Rain cannoned into the side of the house, and thunder rumbled loudly overhead.

I really hate thunder!

Mum's sharp knives were in a block of wood on the kitchen bench. It took a while, but I crawled around the kitchen on my hands and knees to the bench and found the biggest knife. Then I held that out in front of me for protection. I'd be ready for any Zombies or monsters that tried to mess with me.

Next stop was the pantry for some garlic to keep the Vampires away. I wanted something to reveal the ghosts. Flour would do the job, but do you think there was any in the cupboard?

Ripped off!

I slowly crawled along the floor to the study so I could see if anything was hiding under the table and chairs. I took my time to thoroughly check everything properly and quietly.

There were noises. You know, the sort of things that go 'bump' in the night, in the middle of a ferocious storm, when the lights are not working. I didn't know if they were outside or inside the house.

The stairs began creaking like they do when someone walks on them. I thought to myself that I was glad I'd gone to the toilet upstairs because this would be a bad time to remember that you needed to go to the toilet.

Dad's laptop was sitting on his desk. It was normally closed, but I could see it was open. That meant it was turned on, and I could send a message to someone for help and find out why the lights were out.

Guess what?

The laptop wasn't working. It was unplugged and obviously had gone flat. Crap!

Mum and Dad charge their mobile phones in their bedroom. I would have to creep back up the stairs to reach them. If only I'd checked them when I went to the toilet. Those were the only phones in the house because my phone was in the shop being fixed after someone broke it at school a couple of days earlier.

I crawled along the floor to the hallway and waited to see if anything was on the stairs.

I watched light filtering through a window next to the front door. Suddenly, a shadowy figure drifted across that very same window. It looked like an extremely thin man carrying a long knife. The rain was blurring the image. I thought he was saying something, but the wind whistling through a gap in the door drowned out his voice.

The figure started to bang on the front door.

Wide-eyed, I ran from the study and up the stairs two at a time. Why I looked behind myself, I'll never know. But there at the window was the thin man flashing a light into the room. Was he laughing or not? I couldn't tell over the noise of the storm. The light was flashing around the room, so he didn't see me on the stairs.

I was running for my life, as fast as I could, to grab a phone and call for help before he broke in and attacked me. I tripped on the stairs in the dark and as I fell onto the next step, I dropped the knife and put my hand out to break my fall, just like the woman does in the movies before the killer jumps on her and, well, kills her.

I tried not to cry. I wanted to be brave like my dad, but it really hurt, and tears rolled down my cheeks as I sobbed. I knew my wrist was broken, but the doctor later told me that the adrenaline rushing through my veins numbed the pain.

Imagine this. There I was, curled up on the step, cradling my arm and trying not to make a sound, when another lightning flash exposed a moving shadow downstairs, near the front door. I don't know how I did it, but I ignored the pain in my wrist, scrambled up the rest of the stairs to the landing, tiptoed to my mum and dad's room. I didn't see any monsters, but a loud bang outside told me where they were. Or was it thunder? I really, really hate thunder.

I reached the door, which I'd left open and was now shut. I wasn't going in there without the knife I'd dropped on the stairs, so I tiptoed back to where I'd dropped it. 'Oh no, ' I thought. The wind or thunder must have blocked out the sound of the man breaking in. A strong, cold wind was now blowing up the stairs. There were no monsters, but I could still see the man's shadows on the wall. He must've broken a window to get in.

I knew the man was in the house. I didn't know where the monsters and ghosts were. Why were they so quiet when they should've been running around, making a racket and scaring the man away?

I retrieved the knife and quickly crept back to the bedroom, where I shoved open the door as hard as I could to surprise anything there. I could see the bedside tables and wanted the world to swallow me up.

The phones were gone.

I heard more noises downstairs. I couldn't be sure, but I thought the knives on the bench had fallen on the floor.

The bathroom door was open. Of course! Talcum powder! Mum uses talcum powder for all sorts of things. It was in the bathroom cupboard.

I carefully spread it over the floor outside the bedroom to catch any footprints, but the wind blew it everywhere.

Bugger!

I heard another creaking noise, like when a door needs oiling. A tune unknown to me was being whistled. Maybe that's the language monsters use when they talk to each other? To me, they were saying, "She's in the main bedroom, wait till she comes out and we'll grab her!"

Was it the cold, or was it that I was frightened? I shuddered and looked for somewhere to hide. I have no idea what to do to protect yourself from monsters you cannot see. Mum and Dad's wardrobe seemed scarier than hiding under their bed. The monsters were probably waiting there too.

I took a deep breath and edged towards the bed, when I swear, hands on heart, this is the truth. A bodyless voice said "Oi. Find you own hiding place; this place is mine!" Several other voices agreed. Well, let me tell you, I was out of there without looking, and into the cupboard quicker than flies on a dung heap.

As soon as I pulled the door open to the wardrobe, a short ghost wailed and passed through the wall, whilst a bigger ghost disappeared through the floor. A third, larger ghost shot through the roof, realised it was in the rain, returned, screamed at me standing frozen in the doorway, and followed the first ghost through the wall.

I dropped the knife, dived under the bedcovers, pulled the blanket over my head and made sure my arms and legs weren't hanging out – remember? If you leave an arm or leg hanging out of the bed, there's a 75% increase in the chance that monsters will grab them. I hate to think what they'd do if they got hold of me. I didn't want whatever was outside to come in and see me either.

There was yelling downstairs and lots of noise. Maybe the monsters were fighting each other? Maybe they were fighting the unknown intruder? Or maybe they were just clumsy and knocking over furniture? The fighting seemed to last a long time. Then there were several bangs, like gunshots.

Crunch! The bedroom door slammed shut. Had the ghosts or monsters shut me in the bedroom? I wanted to peek, but I was too scared. My heart was racing, my wrist was hurting, and I wanted to cry because of the pain.

More noises downstairs suggested something was in the house. I couldn't help myself; I peeped over the covers. The bedroom door handle was moving. My eyes grew wider the more the handle turned. My heart raced, and chills shot across my body. I was frozen with fear. I wanted to scream, but I knew that's what the females do in those horror movies before they die. I didn't want to die, so I pulled the covers up to my eyes as the door swung open and my wrist exploded in pain.

There, floating off the floor, was a big light. I remember being told not to go towards the light, but the light was coming towards me.

Surely, the intruder, monsters or ghosts had found me.

I screamed. No, I cried out in pain because I was

holding the covers with my sore wrist. I tried to pull them over my head, but the pain was the worst I'd ever felt. I'd given myself away. The intruder or the monsters had found me.

I was gonna die!

The light shone in my face.

I couldn't see who was behind that light, but I knew the voice. "Jenny, are you ok?" Mum asked in a worried way that only mums do when they are concerned. She ran to the bed, and I cried with relief. We hugged and cried. Dad followed Mum in and checked the room. There was nothing there as far as he could see, but I knew better. He stood by the bed next to me and my mum as I told them what happened. Mum looked at my wrist, strapped it and made a sling to hang my arm around my neck because I needed to go to the hospital.

Where had they been all night?

I told you dad was a policeman and mum a nurse. After I'd gone to sleep, they'd received a call about a car crashing into a pole down the road, bringing down power lines and plunging the neighbourhood into darkness in the middle of the storm. They grabbed their phones, torches, and other supplies and rushed out the door, leaving Dad's computer unplugged. They thought that I'd sleep through it all after the effort it took to get me to sleep, so they decided to leave me where I was.

The car belonged to a man who was running away from a family he'd just killed. He thought our house was safe enough to break into and hide. He had a big fight with my dad and another policeman downstairs when they followed his trail of damage to the house. The bangs were a gunfight he lost with my dad and the other policeman.

I still have nightmares about that night, but Mum and Dad are always there to protect and comfort me. The doctor has given me tablets to help me sleep, and the counselling is helping, but I still need a light on at night. I even asked about having friends stay for a sleepover and my parents said yes. Can you believe it, after all that happened, they are happy to let you all stay over? They say it will help me to do that.

It felt great to get the plaster removed from my arm. The doctors said I'll never know that I broke it. Mum was pleased that I didn't miss any school, unfortunately!

Then, lighting struck again and worse than a loud crack of thunder overhead (Did I tell you I really hate thunder?), would you believe it? the man came back!

Only now he's dead and has been haunting our house for the past few months. He makes all sorts of things go bump in the night and has forced the monsters to move out, even the ones that hide under the bed. I haven't seen him, but I often hear him bumping his way through the house and whistling that tune. I sometimes find small objects that have been moved in my room. I know he's watching and trying to hurt me. At night, I hear him saying he's gonna get me. He says I ruined his life, and he will ruin mine as soon as he can figure out how to move bigger objects.

But I didn't do anything. Sure, I was home, but he never saw me.

I think the ghosts or monsters told him something. I reckon he wants to hurt my dad more because of what he did to him. Yet dad won't admit to me that there are ghosts haunting the house, trying to scare him and mum to death.

Nobody believes me!

I finally met a ghost last week. I'd just been to the toilet and was in the bathroom washing my hands. Some funny noises were coming from the wall. Dad said it was just the plumbing, but I knew better. Anyway, the ghost poked its head through the wall and scared me so badly that I, well, let's just say I was scared.

It was scary at first, but then I was disappointed that the ghost was just a regular, run-of-the-mill ghost. You know, white all over, two black holes for eyes, two small holes for a nose and a big hole where the mouth should be. The head was shaped like a head, but the rest of the body was a white sheet. I think someone in the past invented the look of a ghost because they'd met this one.

After the shock of learning ghosts are real, the ghost told me that the other ghosts hadn't moved out yet. Do you know how scary it is to learn that there is not just one ghost in the house, but a lot of them?

The bad man who was killed in the gunfight with my dad and the police is now wanted by the ghost police. I didn't even know that there were ghost police. I mean, what do they do? Arrest ghosts for making too much noise at night? How about not making enough noise? Come on!

To tell the truth, I'm glad that there are ghost police. They even carry a badge. Go figure? They won't tell me much more about what they do or how they do it because it's a case of "The less you know, the less you can get into trouble for." Like that was ever gonna stop me!

The man who died is the new ghost who scared the monsters away. The man is so angry at my family for making him die. He wants to harm us all and won't let the other ghosts and monsters do anything to stop him. So, he forced the monsters to move away and is trying to make the ghosts leave, too.

He doesn't want to become the ghost he is. I know a few people like that – they aren't comfortable being who they really are and try to be something else. Anyway, the other ghosts in the house have been avoiding him because he scares them. They have nowhere else to go. They complained to the ghost police, who came, checked out the house have built a case against him over the past few months.

This must be the weirdest part of this whole story. When things get hard for a ghost, who can they call? Ghost bust, er, police! Anyway, the ghost police arrived four nights ago to talk to me. They found me in bed. I wasn't too scared because I knew they were coming. The other ghost told me what to expect. They sat on the end of the bed, and the ghost in charge asked the questions whilst other ghosts wrote down my answers. They asked me about the night the man died. They were also interested in what he's been saying and doing to me since then.

Other police ghosts wandered the house gathering evidence. When they came back two nights ago, they told about me their plan to catch the intruder because he is hiding from them. I didn't know a ghost could hide from other ghosts.

The ghost police have no issues with what the man says and does to me. That's because he is doing what a ghost is supposed to do. It's the horrible stuff he's been doing to the monsters and other ghosts which is of concern to them. I'd love to know what he's supposed to have done. It can't be easy to scare, threaten or harm creatures that scare people. Unfortunately, they won't tell me what it is that he's supposed to have done. You know why? The less I know, blah, blah, blah! I guess that'll remain a mystery.

Dad admitted that there has been a lot more noise throughout the house in the past few days and he isn't sure what it is but says he'll have a thorough look over the weekend.

This is the ghost police's plan. Tomorrow night, when Mum and Dad are out celebrating their wedding anniversary, I will be at my friend's house. That's when the ghost police will raid my house and catch this intruder. They have all night to do it because Mum and Dad plan to stay at a hotel in the city. I hope they take him away, and I never see or hear from him again. The chief police ghost says that there may be a lot of noise for a while when they arrest the intruder. He says there will be a few things moved, but nothing major to be concerned about, and there will definitely not be any damage to the house.

After that, I won't mind if the monsters move back. I'm no longer scared of them. After all, they were scared away by a ghost that didn't scare me. Well, didn't scare me that much. I've not met a monster, so I don't know what they look like. I think that the ghosts will introduce us because we can learn quite a lot from each other.

Think about that for an experience! Now you know what really happened to my wrist, why I now sleep with a light on in my room, why I'm always tired and have bags under my eyes, and why my mum and dad have the biggest, best alarm system for the house.

Who wants to have a sleepover at my place tonight?

THE END

BAMBOOZLED
By Lisa H Owens

The knock at the front door came early, and Madge nudged George awake, "Get the door; will ya, hon?"

George mumbled something about it still being dark out and rolled over, his snoring picking up where it left off. Madge sat on the edge of the bed, rubbing the sleep from her eyes while Mr. Fluff purred and snaked around her ankles.

"I know Mr. Fluff. I know, love; it woke me up too," she stood and stretched. Her old joints cracked and moaned in protest as she slipped on her bathrobe. An insistent pounding on the door hurried her along.

"Christ A'mighty," George croaked, rolling out of bed to slip on his tennis shorts.

The pounding persisted, and Madge hung back. George approached the door and the knocking ceased. He pressed his eye to the peephole. No one was there.

"Odd," he said, scratching the bald spot on the crown of his head. In the orderly world of West-Coast Sunset Bay, a planned community, this was odd indeed.

He decided the best course of action was to open the door. The sun was cresting the distant hills, casting points of light and shadows on a small cardboard box set upon the front stoop. He stepped outside. Some of the husbands had congregated on the green space at the end of Sunny Circle, as they always did when out-of-the-ordinary events had them scratching their heads. They each held a small box and were having a loud discussion.

"Wait here, Madge," George said, stooping to pick up the box, noticing *Happy Birthday!* Written in thick block letters on the top flap, which lacked an address and postage. Its sides were perforated with pinpricks. Air holes, George thought and tapped the cleft in his chin. He knew it wasn't his birthday, and momentarily panicked. He did a quick mental calculation, then smiled. Madge's birthday was in June, two months away.

Nearly weightless, the box felt empty. He lightly shook it and could feel something shift inside. Box in hand, he walked to join the men, the breadwinners of their respective families, in the green space. Additional men, in various stages of undress, and a woman named Betty, whose husband always seemed to be on a business trip, staggered alongside George, carrying boxes.

As they neared, George caught snippets of perplexed conversation. *What do you think... Who sent... air holes… not my birthday… empty… some kind of prank…*

"Hear! Hear!" Sully Peterson called the group to order. His family had lived on Sunny Circle the longest, and he was the elected head of the neighbourhood watch and homeowners' association, a fact he pointed out at every opportunity.

"As elected head of the neighbourhood watch and homeowners' association…" sighs of exasperation ensued as eyes rolled, and he briefly paused to glare at the offenders before proceeding. "I want to say, *very funny.* Without a doubt, this goes against the HOA bylaws. Who's the wise guy here, waking us at the crack of dawn on a Saturday, and what's the dealio with the boxes, Daddy-O?"

George piped up, "Perhaps it's someone's birthday. My box says *Happy Birthday!*" he turned the box sideways for all to see, "but it's neither mine nor Madge's birthday."

"You sure about that, Georgie?" A voice rang out, the tension broke for a moment as the men had a good laugh at George's expense. He'd been in the doghouse on more than one occasion for forgetting things—important things—like birthdays and anniversaries.

"No, really," he said, turning to wave at Madge, looking for support in this matter, but she had gone inside, hopefully to brew a pot of strong coffee.

Boxes were held high, and the crowd grew quiet. *Happy Birthday!* in identical block letters was penned atop every box.

"As elected head of the neighbourhood…"

Gary interrupted, "Give it a rest, would ya? Believe me, you never let us forget it. So, Mr. Sully Peterson—elected head of the neighbourhood watch—did ya happen to *watch* who put the boxes on the stoops?"

Sully stared at the ground. "Well… no, but in my defence, it was still dark when our doorbell rang."

The men and Betty studied their own boxes. Some held them up, allowing the early morning sunlight to shine through the tiny pinholes, in hopes of spying something inside, and others lightly shook them. Speculations came fast and furious. *Money? A dust bunny? Stale air? Explosives?*

The housewives of Sunny Circle, still adorned in sponge curlers, fuzzy bathrobes and bunny slippers, watched the dilemma unfold from their front stoops.

A lone voice rang out from a distant stoop—one of the wives—silencing all others, "Open them for Pete's sake!"

The men and Betty turned to face Pete, a quiet fellow standing on the outskirts of the group, and he blushed. All eyes were on the shy young man.

"Well?" Sully nodded at Pete.

"I don't think she meant it literally," Pete's cheeks turned a deeper shade of red, as he extracted a Swiss Army Knife from the pocket of his wrinkled khaki slacks, obviously Friday's work pants hastily pulled from the dirty clothes hamper. He opened the blade. The husbands and Betty stepped back to give Pete a wide berth, echoes of the word *explosives* still ringing in their ears. Pete held the box in his palm while he worked the tip of the blade under the cellophane tape sealing the top. His hands trembled, and he nearly dropped it.

"Oh, for God's sake; give it here," said Betty. She swiped the knife from his shaky hand and, in one swift motion, sliced the strip of tape on his box. The men cradled their own boxes, stepping back even further.

"KABOOM," one of the wives shouted from the safety of her porch, and a nervous titter rippled around the cul-de-sac.

Pete steadied his hands and held the box as Betty carefully peeled back the flaps of cardboard. She leaned over to peer inside.

"Why, it's a plant," she cried, handing her unopened box to Gary. She used two expertly manicured fingernails to pull out a bundle of tiny green shoots, held together by a wiry root ball. The group closed in.

"There's a note," Pete reached inside to retrieve a slip of folded paper as the husbands, and Betty, ripped the tape from their own boxes to find identical small bundles with folded notes beneath them.

Sully read his note aloud in a booming voice to remind the group that he was important:

"Today is my birthday; I am Lucky Bamboo.
Plant me in your garden without much ado.
Water me plenty; never let me go dry.
You'll be amazed how I multiply."

They all had the same message. Identical back-slanted cursive handwriting (the author obviously a lefty). Pete flipped his empty box over to find a series of ink-stamped Chinese characters and a smiling panda bear, identifying China as the package's origin.

Sully looked around at the confused expressions on his neighbours' faces and snarled, "Dirty Commie bastards," storming off. He lifted the metal lid on his trash barrel to drop the box along with the bamboo sprig and note on top of a bulging bag of trash.

"Good riddance," he shouted from his front porch, placing a meaty palm on his wife's lower back to guide her inside the house. He dusted off his hands and slammed the front door.

The slam of the door snapped the crowd into action, and they scattered. The husbands carried their plants, handing them off to the housewives, who in turn, handed their men steaming hot cups of coffee.

Except for Betty. Since her husband always seemed to be "on a business trip," she went it alone, and had already calculated the perfect spot to plant the baby bamboo. She would call him Little Arnie, after her husband, Big Arnold, and plant him in the freshly tilled and mulched flowerbed along the back fence.

***

Clad in gardening attire, Betty sat on the ground in front of the flowerbed, still lacking flowers or plants of any kind. From the look of things, Arnold's boxer-mix had spent another morning digging out the centre of the bed. Trowel in hand, she would perform another, in an endless series of *fill-ins* on Boomer's untidy holes. Boomer was a real pain in her derriere lately, always digging in that same spot. Little Arnie was laid out on the grass beside her, prepped and ready to go into the ground. He would be the first addition to her garden. Betty returned the displaced soil to Boomer's hole and smoothed it over before trying Little Arnie in various areas of the prepared soil. His placement within the bed must be perfect. Maybe a little to the left and back a smidge.

She laid her palm atop the spot and closed her eyes in concentration. She felt *him*. Felt his perpetual befuddlement, as he lay rotting beneath the soil. Big Arnold's upturned face should be right… here. She used a trowel to dig a hole twice the size of the bamboo sprig's root ball, added a pinch of root stimulator, a dash of water, and centred Little Arnie in the hole. She sang the words of the poem as she covered his roots in topsoil, then turned the hose on him:

"Water me plenty; never let me go dry.
You'll be amazed how I multiply."

A low growl resonated from deep within Boomer's chest as Betty sang and Little Arnie hummed and swayed, his roots sucking up the moisture as fast as it flowed from the hose.

"Somebody's thirsty," Betty giggled and increased the water-flow rate. Little Arnie's tiny stalks grew a bit taller.

Boomer cut loose with a series of groans and barks when she turned the nozzle to an even higher rate of flow, and she silenced him with a spritz of the tepid water.

"Hush, puppy," she frowned at her use of the southern-fish-fry pun. She sounded like Big Arnold. When did she adopt his lame attempts at humour?

Disgusted, she sent a deluge of water over the edge

of the flowerbed, dousing Little Arnie good. Wiry roots snaked from beneath the saturated soil, and Boomer's damp fur bristled. Betty's lips curled up in a demented smile, and she twisted the nozzle a quarter-turn to jet spray. She blasted the roots. Little Arnie squeaked and with a moist squelch, he was sucked beneath the soil. Maniacal laughter filled the air as Betty lost all self-control, wielding the hose like a weapon and roots flew over and through the backyard—weaving in and out of the soil like a basting stitch on a runaway sewing machine. Thousands of Little Arnie's erupted from the carpet of vines criss-crossing the entire perimeter of the yard, ending just shy of the privacy fence. The sun broke over the roofline of Betty's cookie-cutter home, and bright green shoots of bamboo pulsated as they rapidly lengthened. It was at this point that Betty's lucidity returned, and she knew they were in trouble.

Betty dropped the hose, shouting "Run, Boomer," and side-by-side, the duo sprinted toward the back deck.

***

The packing room of the warehouse was a hub of activity as the bots worked side-by-side preparing the boxes. In unison, they performed their duties. Eight hundred left hands morphed into *quills* to pen the poem. The vinyl-polymer hands worked at a rapid pace, morphing into the tools necessary to complete each task before sealing the boxes with cellophane tape. Nearing the end of the process, the hands morphed one last time. In unison, eight hundred stamps clicked the bottoms of eight hundred boxes, leaving behind the corporate name—*Lucky Bamboo, Incorporated*—and logo, a smiling panda. Multiple layers of boxes, stacked floor to ceiling by a horde of gangly crane-bots, aligned the west end of the warehouse. Westward bound, the bamboo sprigs would bring luck and new beginnings. The next shipment of *Happy Birthday!* boxes were ready to cross the oceans blue on one of many corporate freightliners.

***

The residents of Sunset Bay met the following morning for their monthly *tidy-up, the green space meet and greet* in the Sunny Circle cul-de-sac. They would also take a vote on what to do with the tiny bundles of bamboo. A sprig of bamboo on its own wouldn't make an impact on one's yard. It would get lost among the lush flora and fauna already adorning the lawns of the proud homeowners. The thought of planting all of the sprigs in the green space for maximum effect was high on the list, but *what to do with the bamboo* was the second item on the group of neighbours' agenda.

The first item was to find Sully, their fearless leader. Morning phone calls to his house had gone unanswered, which was completely out of character. He had never missed an opportunity to assert his authority as an elected official in a group setting. Overseeing the monthly Sunday beautifying of the green space was the highlight of his life, since he and Judy had joined the ranks of empty-nesters. Madge led the wives in laying out the various gardening tools while the husbands walked the short distance to Sully and Judy's house. They righted his flipped-over trash barrel, replaced the putrid bag of trash and clapped on the metal lid.

"What in the Sam Hill?" George murmured as the group followed a snaking trail of wiry roots across the driveway, up the stoop and to the front door, where they had infiltrated a narrow crevice at its base.

"Come on out, Sully, ya old bastard," George, having deemed himself temporary leader, shouted as he rang the doorbell. Silence prevailed beyond the door.

"I'll check the back," Gary called over his shoulder, rounding the corner of the house.

They heard the creak of hinges as Gary opened the gate and then insistent knocking on the back door.

The hinges creaked again as Gary emerged from the backyard.

"I don't think they're home," George deduced, scratching his bald spot.

The group of husbands stared at one another for a few moments. Sure. They loved to tease him, but Sully had always been the organizer where things regarding the neighborhood were concerned. His catch phrase, "Chaos begets chaos," graced his lips on a regular basis.

"Should we carry on without the old man?" George asked, drumming his fingers on his forehead.

Sully and Judy Peterson, in earshot of the ongoing dilemma, did not respond. They sat on the floral chintz sofa in the formal living room. It was rare for them to sit there, on the crystal-clear vinyl sofa cover—a wedding gift from Great Aunt Ruth, meant to protect the expensive fabric—unless they were entertaining guests. Shafts of light poured in through the lace curtains Judy had sewn on her handy-dandy Singer sewing machine in earlier years, when the Sunset Bay planned community had seemed to appear overnight. In the early 60s, new homes were built in a frenzy as the population of the West Coast exploded. The vacant eyes of the man and his bride of nearly thirty years stared out through the aged lace curtains covering the front window of the happy home in which they'd raised two children, as slump-shouldered, the men stepped off the front stoop to rejoin their wives in the green space.

A small box flecked with brain matter sat in Sully's lap. *Happy Birthday!* On its open lid was partially obscured by crusty gore. From within the box, thin roots threaded upwards to end at clusters of jagged bamboo shoots, protruding through the foreheads and eye-sockets of he and his beloved wife.

Just a stone's throw away, the Sunny Circle wives served the Sunday morning Bloody Marys, and the men prepared to mow and weed-eat the green space.

"Hey," Madge stopped mid-pour, "Where's Betty?"

***

Betty and Boomer had spent Saturday night on the back deck. Betty had sprawled out on a chaise lounge chair, and though he was too big, Boomer curled up in her lap. The brilliance of the full moon in the wee hours of Sunday morn cast an otherworldly glow on the thousands of bamboo shoots filling the backyard's every nook and cranny. The wind stirred a throaty *hoo-hoo* as it brushed over the hollow tip of each stalk, conducting a macabre, reedy symphony.

Neither Betty nor Boomer drew solace from the eerie

music. Betty's lips were forever locked in a tortured grimace, her hand resting atop Boomer's rigid head, the two of them skewered through and through, like meat-kabobs on bamboo skewers. The bamboo swayed, its collective mass overtaxing the dog-eared cedar boards of the perimeter fence. Water from the gushing hose saturated the lawn, seeping under and beyond the property line, and the fence creaked and groaned with each shift of the wind. Big Arnold's decaying head, ensconced in a low thatch of bamboo, hovered above the flowerbed. The Sunday morning sun awoke, warming matted clumps of Big Arnold's hair, and the decomposing skin on his face glistened.

***

The entire Sunset Bay community, less Betty and the Peterson's—the trio's uncharacteristic absence a mystery—celebrated the successful planting of the bamboo in the green space on Sunny Circle. A new name and its designation as an official park was still pending Sully's approval, but that was merely a formality. The Peterson's would love having a neighborhood park adjacent to their home—especially once grandkids came along.

Overnight, Pete, quite the handyman, constructed a

sign. He painted the background white with *LUCKY BAMBOO PARK* stencilled across in green block letters.

What a pleasant surprise to receive the Happy Birthday! boxes, Pete thought. Their neighbourhood would forever be the first of its kind, known for its luscious bamboo park. The boxes were trending. His younger sister Autumn lived on the opposite side of the country in East Coast Sunrise Harbour, one of a myriad of newly constructed planned communities. The entire neighbourhood had been awakened to disarray in a similar manner, *Happy Birthday!* Boxes set upon their front stoops.

Pete watched the neighborhood kids play a vicious game of Red-Light Green-Light in the Peterson's side yard while awaiting their turns to put their marks on the sign. One-by-one he called them over. Each kid dipped the palm of one hand in sunshine yellow paint, then pressed it against the white base paint. Dozens of yellow palm prints of varying sizes surrounded and highlighted the green block letters.

Pete let the handprints dry as he dug and filled a deep hole with wet cement in a patch of grass in the foreground of what would become the new park entrance. Then, he centred the sign, secured to a treated pine stake, in the concrete to let it set up before covering the area with topsoil and grass seed. George and Gary, who had supervised a team of willing husbands in installing rotating sprinkler heads around the perimeter of the green space, were just wrapping things up. Bamboo needed a moist environment to thrive.

The work complete, George shouted, "Crank it up, Madge!"

The sprinkler heads burst to life, just as the afternoon sun emerged from behind a curtain of lacy white clouds. The sprigs of bamboo began to hum and sway.

***

Mad scientist *He Jiankui's* great-grandson, *He Hung,* cut loose an evil laugh, befitting one of many in a long line of mad scientists, as he stamped the paperwork authorising the termination of Project Panda. The do-gooder conservation plan that had been initiated in China during the severe deforestation of bamboo in the mid-1900s was no longer necessary. The mad scientist and his crew of bots would soon rule a bamboo world, void of people.

THE END

Memoriae
By Jonathan J Bowerman

The small, plain room in the library was dark and musty, and on all accounts fairly unremarkable. A window on the far wall hung open, but there was no breeze to stir the stale air. A solid wooden door opened slowly…reluctantly.

"Come in and have a seat," said a dark figure, who was sitting in a chair behind an ornate oak desk; the only detailed thing in the room. "Tell me, what do you remember?" the man asked his young apprentice.

A young girl of about ten years plopped down in a small office chair. Her attitude revealed her age. "Oh, master, why must we go over this every night?"

"Celia, what do you remember?" His patience never swayed.

She huffed. "I remember doing this last night, and the night before, and the night before, and–"

"It is important." His voice was direct, but not harsh. "My time is almost up, but yours has not even begun. You must be prepared, or I will have failed." The dark figure interlaced his fingers and set his hands on the desk. The chair creaked gently underneath his shifting weight.

Celia forfeited and tried to recollect the memories of the day she'd had. "I remember waking up *way* too early." She opened one eye and glared at her master with it.

"And?"

She continued. "I remember breakfast."

"What did you have?"

Again, she huffed. "Cereal. Stale cereal, actually."

"Continue."

"I remember my chores."

"What ch–"

She interrupted with an attitude that could melt the coldest ice. "Sweeping, mopping, doing the dishes. The typical *Cinderella* stuff."

"Continue."

Somewhere in the room, they heard a small mouse scurrying across the floor. It stopped, squeaked, then continued until they heard it no more. Outside, not too far off, they heard a large bird diving from its high limb, no doubt an owl catching its breakfast.

Celia's master pushed himself up from his chair and started around the desk toward his apprentice. "Continue, *please*, Celia."

She rambled off the rest of her day. "I remember going to school, almost getting in a fight with a bully…

again. Coming home, eating dinner, and now here we are."

"Good, but not great. What colour was your breakfast bowl? How hot was the dish water? What colour socks did the bully have on? How many peas were on your dinner plate? And finally, how far did you have to open the door to get inside, and how long did I wait until I told you to have a seat?"

Celia hung her head in defeat. "I don't know."

"Last thing. This afternoon, when you connected with the mouse's memories. What did you see?"

"Not much. There were a lot of noises I didn't understand, some scratching and nest building, and he got extremely excited when he found some crumbs in the kitchen."

"Good," her master said with a smile. "That's about the extent of it. That is what I gathered, too. Remember, you are simply honing your connecting skills. You need to work on that more than anything else."

"Master, I don't understand why this is so important."

"It's *very* important," he began, while still approaching her, "because it will mean life or death in the very near future. All the little details–from colours to time, and distance to smells–will assist you in doing what you must." He stopped behind her. "Now," he said, putting his hands on her shoulders, "let us return."

Instantly, the room erupted into a crescendo of deep, ground-shaking vibrations. Red, yellow, and blue ribbons of light splashed onto the walls and wrapped around the two of them. Celia squeezed her eyes tighter and white-knuckle gripped the arms of the chair until it creaked in protest. Her master had travelled this way hundreds of times, but she, only a few.

Just when it seemed like the world around them would crumble, they warped out of the study and into a small room with copper-lined walls. Little shapes and figurines hung from the ceiling, and shimmering crystals encircled them on the floor. The splash of colours faded, and the vibration stopped.

"Good job, Celia, but you must try harder," he whispered before picking his unconscious apprentice up and carrying her out of the room. A small cot waited for her down one of the halls of 217 Silverworm Lane–one of four secret headquarters of the infiltration group known merely as *Memoriae*. Unlike any other infiltration group, though, they infiltrated people's minds. A large glass of water was all Celia's master required after their training and warp back to reality. He downed it in a single gulp.

"Bruce?" A voice came from the end of the hall. "You're back. What took you so long?"

"I told you these things require time and patience. I

cannot simply snap my fingers and have an apprentice trained up the way you and your bosses want them to be. Please understand."

The other man now stood in front of him. He leaned in close. "Time is what we don't have," he said in a hushed tone. "If I ask my bosses for even one more week, they will ring my neck and yours too."

"I'd like to see them try."

The man relaxed his shoulders. "Look, we all know you're the best memory detective we have, and an exceptional wizard at that, but you've got to try and see things from our perspective. Whether you like it or not, your time is almost up. They will want to use Celia."

At the mention of his apprentice's name, he finally showed some form of emotion. "She is not ready." He growled. "If you plant her into one of these maniacs before I say so, they will eat her alive."

"It's out of my hands."

"You better put it back *in* your hands, or else." The man started walking down the hall. "She's not ready!" he shouted. The man shrugged his shoulders and kept walking. Bruce looked back at his apprentice, still passed out on the cot.

One week later

"Good, very good! You have grown leaps and bounds, Celia. Now, how about the floorboards in the kitchen? How many were there?" Bruce was sitting in the same study and in the same chair he had been a week ago. He was looking at his young apprentice and questioning her about her day.

"Twenty-seven, no… twenty-eight," she responded.

"Direction?"

"East to west and each approximately fifteen feet in length."

"Impressive," Bruce said, smiling. "Let's move on to something a little deeper, shall we?"

Celia smirked. "Go for it."

The two had nearly tripled their training time, and Bruce's expectations had doubled. Ceilia was growing, but she was also still immature. That was something her master could not help her with; she would have to learn maturity with age.

"When you first walked into the kitchen, what did you smell?" Bruce asked. He raised his eyebrows.

"The fabrication was cooking. I believe it was a roast–it smelled amazing, by the way–with potatoes, carrots, onions, and celery."

"Herbs?"

"Rosemary, thyme, parsley, salt and pepper, and," she paused for a moment. Something was coming back to her memory that didn't make sense, but she knew it was there.

"And? Go ahead, trust your instincts."

"Ummm, ok, well, there was also… peanut butter, vinegar, and cinnamon?" She screwed up her face at the disgusting and uncommon combination.

"Very good." He giggled. "You will learn that there are times our minds try to make us forget something simply because it deems the memory illogical or unreasonable. With experience, you will be able to control what you forget and don't forget. That was a test, and you passed with flying colours. What about the dogs outside?"

"There were three, and they were all carrying on about the very same smells. I think they thought it was for them."

"Good. Now–" Celia's master stopped and listened to the voice that was echoing inside his head. "I am sorry, but our training is over for the day. They are calling us back." He stood up and walked behind Celia as he'd done before. The vibration and colours began. Moments later, they were in the copper-lined room. Celia was nearly used to travelling by now, but still felt queasy for a while afterwards.

"I'm going for a lie down, master." Celia left the room and headed for the cot.

The shady man from the other day was waiting in the doorway. "Well done, Celia," he said. His tone was sugar-coated, but with a hint of vinegar. His words always seemed complimentary, but something about them was superficial. "Well done." He smiled at her and tried to pat her on the head, but she ducked just out of reach.

"What is it? Why did you interrupt our training?" Bruce had just downed his glass of water.

"I'm sorry, but I tried."

"You tried? You tried what?"

The man glanced over his shoulder to ensure Celia had put some distance between her and them. "They won't listen to me anymore. They are going to use Celia tonight."

"But they–" suddenly Bruce's body stiffened and he could not move. Like a stone statue he fell forward onto the ground.

"The… water…"

The man bent over and whispered into Bruce's ear. "I apologise, old friend, but we couldn't have you mucking things up for us. It's nothing personal, strictly business." Still squatting, he spoke into a radio: "Move in and take the girl."

Moments later, the two heard Celia screaming. Muscular men wearing black suits were hauling her into another room. Bruce struggled to move, but struggle was all he did. "I'll kill you. I'll kill ALL of you," he growled through clenched teeth.

"I know, but we feel once you see that she is ready, this will all be water under the bridge. We–" he stopped. "Bruce?" He nudged him with his boot. "Hmm, out already? That stuff *is* potent." He started down the hallway. "Ok, boys, let's do this. We don't have much time. When Bruce wakes up, he'll be as mad as a hornet's nest."

The man entered the room and saw that the two large men had already used wide leather straps to immobilise Celia to a chair. She jerked her head back and forth before they strapped that to the chair, too. Like a cornered wolf, she snapped at their fingers.

"Now, now, little girl," the man began, "you may be Bruce's favourite, but to us you're just another pawn. We need you to be cooperative and show us what you're capable of. Do you think you can manage that?"

Celia spat at him, then a thick, feverish fear washed over her as the man snapped his fingers and one of the large men raised a needle into the air just in Celia's view. He pushed the plunger slightly until a bright yellow liquid squirted out of it.

"That's better," the man said. "Now will you cooperate?" Celia nodded. "Good." He picked up his radio again. "Bring in prisoner number four." Two other large men dragged in a scrawny, desperate fellow with a five o'clock shadow and nasty yellow teeth. He too struggled, but was just as successful as Celia.

Celia thought it funny that deep down inside, she felt a tinge of empathy for the man, for they were both in the same predicament. That was until she saw the familiar number tattoo on his neck, indicating that he was a prisoner of the worst kind. She snarled and was disgusted to even be in his presence.

The man took one look at her, eyed her up and down, then licked his lips. A distasteful "mmmmm" gurgled from the back of his repulsive throat.

"Strap him in," the shady man said, pointing to an empty chair with his radio hand. The chair was directly across from Celia. It could be two states away, and it would still be too close for her comfort. "Hurry up," he continued, "we don't have much time."

Celia could smell 'number four.' It was not pleasant. It smelled like he hadn't showered in a month. She turned her head in an attempt to avoid the thick, repugnant odour.

Without command, one of the men approached the prisoner and drove a needle into his neck and emptied its contents. Seconds later, the man's eyes rolled into the back of his head, and the struggling ceased. If not for the straps, the prisoner would have crumpled to the floor.

"Now, Celia, this is where you come into play. This man here," he pointed to the prisoner in the seat, "he is a very bad man. He is responsible for killing many, many people. The thing is, we don't know where his victims are. We need you to go inside of his memories and shovel through the mess. Find not only where he hid the bodies, but also where he is keeping his other victims. Can you do that?"

A tear rolled down Celia's cheek. "I don't know. I've never actually done this before. Master has been teaching me to work on my focus and attention, but I've only ever connected with animals."

"Nonsense. You've been training with your master for weeks. This is just like training; you can do it. I believe– no, we believe in you. Don't we boys?" The large men nodded supportively, but Celia wasn't buying it. "Besides, this man is as much animal as anything else. Trust me." His tone was supportive and encouraging.

"I'm not a toddler, don't patronise me." Celia snapped.

"Listen to me you little twerp." The man lunged forward and grabbed her mouth. "You're gonna inside of that... *freak's* head and you're gonna find out where the nut-job is keeping all those kids. You understand me?!"

"Kids?" Celia mumbled.

He let go. "Yes, kids. You can do this. Just remember what your master has been teaching you." He motioned for one of the large men to shut the door to the room.

Celia took a moment and collected her thoughts. She closed her eyes and focused on the man sitting next to her. It wasn't that hard for her; she could smell him a mile away and could never forget his face. After a few seconds, her connection was complete. She was looking through his eyes:

A narrow path led up a small hill. Multiple birds were flying and singing their songs (the calls of bluefinches, known to keep to the hills of the west end of Blackfoot Forest). The trees were thin and tall (approximately 30 feet high from ground to tip); they swayed with the breeze (wind speed approximately 5 miles per hour, coming from the south). There was a slight stench in the air (a pulp mill). She watched footsteps until they arrived in front of a run-down cabin with yellow-stained windows and an old door with rusty hinges (sixty-seven steps from road to cabin with a two-and-a-half-foot gate). The man looked over his shoulders a few times before using a key to unlock a padlock (Smith brand key, approximately three-quarters of an inch in length, silver, same brand and colour padlock). It rattled noisily. He shoved the door open and stepped onto creaky boards (seventeen boards, twenty feet long). Pitiful whimpering came from somewhere near the back of the cabin (estimating six separate voices).

He walked to the room and checked on the victims (six children awake, two sleeping, all tied up with cloth bags over their heads). He left the room and proceeded out of the back door (six steps with a two-and-a-half-foot gate). He had his own cemetery (five freshly filled holes, eight waiting to be filled and covered). The man reached down and picked up a shovel, then proceeded to dig more holes.

Everything was going perfectly, at first. Celia was achieving exactly what she had been training for: insight, focus, situational awareness, information, and more. But something began to go wrong. Something didn't feel right. She had felt it once when she connected with a mouse for the very first time. Something inside the mouse began to panic. It was as if the little creature *knew* someone was inside its head. The very same thing started to take place.

Somehow, even in his insensible state of mind, the prisoner knew someone was fishing around inside of their unconsciousness. His mind began to fight back. It tried to cover up its deepest, darkest, little secrets.

In the prisoner's memories, where Celia currently was, a violent wind stirred up. The tall trees began to tremble, creak, and groan. Dirt, leaves, and limbs engulfed Celia's thoughts and threw off her focus. The run-down cabin began to turn in on itself and contort in unrealistic ways to the point that it looked more like a Dali painting than an actual house. The ground gave out underneath her, and she began to fall.

Her master had warned her about it, but at that moment, Celia could not recall the remedy for if she were to find herself in that sort of predicament. Celia, herself, began to panic. If she didn't do something, and do something very quickly, she would be lost inside the mind of a psychopath and lose hers altogether.

Suddenly and without warning, the door to the room where Celia was being kept burst into a thousand tiny shards of wood. The knob and hinges floated in mid-air for a second then shot toward the four guards, landing between their eyes and knocking them unconscious. Bruce burst into the room with ribbons of magic whipping all around him.

"I told you, she was not ready!" His voice was thunderous and powerful. It filled the room like molasses; nothing would escape his anger.

"Now, Bruce–" the shady man began. He was silenced immediately with the flick of a wrist.

Bruce wrenched the chair that the prisoner had been sitting in from the floor. The prisoner flew one way, and the chair flew straight towards the man. It landed on him with a loud thud and then wrapped itself around him as if he were trapped in a grizzly bear's grip. The leather straps wrapped themselves around the chair and the man and held them both in place.

Bruce was breathing, panting with anger, but the state in which he saw his apprentice quenched his rage immediately. He knew she was in trouble. He ran up to her and placed his hands on either side of her face, and closed his eyes.

Celia had been falling in darkness for what seemed like an eternity. Racing up the path, her master dodged around the melting trees, ran through the bulging cabin and dove straight into the abyss-of-a-hole his apprentice had been swallowed up by. He caught up to her, reached out and caught her. Yellow, red, and blue ribbons wrapped around the two of them, and in an instant, everything went black.

Two Days Later

An old television with a bunny-ear antenna and old knobs on its front poured out the most recent news report: "Eight children in all have been located and are recovering at a nearby hospital, but sadly, many more have been found behind the decrepit cabin." A young woman in a professional suit sat behind a desk and spoke into a microphone. "Authorities say an anonymous tip pointed them to this part of the woods," she continued, "which led to a miraculous ending to a witch hunt of a case."

Bruce sat in a deep chair next to the cot that Celia had been sleeping in for the past two days. Her experience left her both physically and mentally drained. Her hand twitched as she finally began to stir. She grumbled and tried to speak. Even the smallest of movements shot red-hot waves of pain through her body.

"Shhh, don't speak," Bruce said. He smiled down at her sympathetically. "You are in no condition to say anything, or even move, for that matter."

"M-master?"

"Yes, it's me. Don't try to open your eyes either. It takes time and a lot of rest when you've made it through a successful connection. Especially one as taxing and dangerous as the one you have."

"You mean I did it?" She groaned. She could feel her heart beating inside her head. The excruciating thud, thud, thud made her wish she was still out.

Bruce laughed lightly. "Yes, you did it. Because of what you accomplished, those eight children will recover and be able to hug their parents once again. For the children who have already died, their parents will have closure. You should be very proud of yourself,

Celia." He gently placed his hand on her shoulder. "Now you rest, I have something to take care of."

Bruce stood and left the room. He walked down the hall and into the main lobby, where three men in expensive suits were waiting. After a quick discussion, they came to an agreement. Bruce would stay with Celia at 217 Silverworm Lane, where he would continue their training. Celia would only go as far as *she* wanted to and would only connect with others when she felt she was ready. Neither she nor Bruce would be under the thumb of his bosses anymore. In exchange for that, Bruce would release his old friend back to them. It turns out he was acting on his own accord and had cost them quite a lot of money. They wanted to be sure he paid for his mistakes.

Bruce walked back into the room where Celia was continuing to recover.

"Is it over?" Celia asked weakly.

"Oh, my dear Celia, I believe it all has just begun."

Fifty-Three Years Later

The small, plain room in the library was dark and musty, and on all accounts fairly unremarkable. A window on the far wall hung open, but there was no breeze to stir the stale air. A solid wooden door opened slowly…reluctantly.

"Come in and have a seat," said a dark figure, who

was sitting in a chair behind an ornate oak desk; the only detailed thing in the room. "Tell me, what do you remember?" she asked her young apprentice.

THE END

FROM THE STARS
By Emil Haskett

Grandma was dead and in the ground. That was how Dad put it. Mom said he talked tough to mask his true feelings. I had seen it before, he got angry or acted indifferent when he was sad.

I was sad. Grandma had always been around. And I hadn't realized that when a person died, it wasn't just the person that was gone. Pancakes, bedtime stories and the smell of lemon soap --all of it disappeared with the person.

October was halfway through; the long, dark winter awaited. Grandma always said, "There is no trouble in the world that hot chocolate can't fix." Grandma fixed my problems often, listening to me, telling ghost stories –and making hot chocolate. It was magic. Countless times I had seen her pour sugar and cocoa into warm cream and then add milk.

"In some cultures," Grandma used to say as she stirred, "they put these ingredients in graves, they thought that when the dead person awoke on the other side they could use a nice, hot cup."

Now Grandma was gone. And so was hot chocolate. My parents couldn't make it like she did. Mom would burn the cream and Dad would only make the store-bought kind, too sweet and lacking the bitter touch of cocoa.

That was when the thing from outer space appeared. I was stuck in my room with my maths homework. Progress was slow. Impossible formulas demanding answers that I didn't know. Something shimmered in the night sky, like a big glistening tear of oil falling. It sped through the night, headed towards my house.

I slammed the book shut and rushed out to meet it.

"Did you finish your homework; you can't go out until you have!" Mom shouted but I was already out the door.

It was huge. A falling black star, crashing through the treetops and down on our lawn.

It was difficult to describe what it looked like. Ever-changing, ever-moving. It kind of reminded me of smoke but it was still solid. It didn't have eyes, but I could tell that it immediately noticed me, or sensed me.

"I am wounded," it said mouthless.

Its voice was old. I don't know how I knew, but some things you just know. This thing had been around. There were rips and scars in the smooth body, purple and crimson tears in the alien fabric. Shimmering fluids oozed through the wounds.

"Have you been in a fight? Tom Wilkins once

punched me in the face. My nose started bleeding."

"I will answer all your questions, but first I need shelter."

It had crashed next to the old henhouse. We had never kept chickens, it was what the old lady who sold the house to us had called it. It was empty now, only a faint lingering scent of fowl and some sprinkles of old hay as a reminder of what had been.

"You can sleep in there. If you can get in, that is."

It was almost the size of the henhouse. It dragged itself over the frostbitten grass. Heavy and slug-like. I opened the door and it slid into the house. It was barely visible in the lightless room.

"Do you need anything?"

"Nourishment," the darkness answered.

I closed the door not really believing that it would keep the alien in but hopefully, it would keep the cat out. The grass shimmered in the moonlight. Fall was Grandma's favourite season. Hot chocolate and cinnamon buns by the fire, maybe a ghost story that my parents wouldn't approve of. I held back a sob, it was as if the vast autumn night opened up the enormous loss of Grandma.

"Now finish your homework!" Dad shouted with arms full of laundry, unaware of my tears.

I ran up the stairs, drying my eyes with the back of

my hand and took the maths book from my desk and returned down to the kitchen. I looked for something to give the alien to eat and decided on the brown paper bag under the sink, full of old apples, bananas, potato peels and leftovers. The fruit flies stirred when I put an empty bag back in the holder.

"I swear to God, go and finish your homework."

"On it, I'll just throw this out first." I was out the door with the book and the bag before he could answer. I walked to the henhouse expecting the alien to be gone and for the whole thing to just be a strange dream.

But in the dark room, it waited. Its body glistened like oil, and the wounds were almost translucent.

I took an apple out of the bag and tossed it, not daring to feed the alien with my hand. I heard no munching, nor the apple hitting the floor or wall. It had just dissolved into the alien.

"More." There was no threat in the voice.

I took a soft, brown banana from the bag and threw it. One of the wounds seemed to close up.

"Who gave you those wounds?"

"Even space has claws." Eyeless, it gazed at me as if sizing me up. "Remember, life is struggle. The key is to continue."

"So, you are like super old?"

"I am as old as the oldest stars. I was here at the

beginning of time. I could answer questions if you want. My knowledge is deep and ancient."

"You know everything? Like Google?"

Silence. Apparently, it didn't know about Google. I looked at the strange creature, an ever-changing mass of oily, dark matter.

"What are you?"

The darkness hesitated, at least that is what I thought it was doing.

"I am," it answered. "As are you."

One of the wounds wasn't oozing anymore, it seemed to have healed.

"Is there something else that you wish to learn?"

"Actually, there is." I said, remembering the book in my hand.

"So, what is your question?"

I opened my maths book, flipping through the pages, there were more of my drawings and scribblings than answers to the maths problems.

"I need help with this one." I held the maths book in front of the pulsating darkness so it could see better.

"I could tell you the secrets of the universe, what the stars dream of, I could…"

"No thanks, just this one please."

"The answer is 64."

"64? Huh, I would never have guessed that." I

scribbled the answer before I forgot it. "And this one?" I said pointing to the next maths problem.

A sound came from the dark thing. Maybe an alien sigh. "Isn't there something else you would rather learn? Lifeforms on other planets? The secret to longevity?"

"No, not really. I need this homework done by tomorrow. I'll give you the rest of this bag of compost if you help me."

The thing quivered. Hungry and yearning for nourishment. I threw the whole bag at it and the paper bag disappeared. Then we worked through the homework, assignment by assignment.

Later that night, my head resting on Grandma's old pillowcase I thought about the strange alien in the henhouse.

***

The next day at school, Mrs Higgins reluctantly approved of my progress. I could sense her suspicion as she glared at my homework. But she didn't ask if my parents helped me. In the following weeks, I kept feeding the alien and it kept helping me with my homework. It had the answer for almost everything, the only time it remained silent was when I had to write an essay about the British royal family, of that, it had nothing to say.

It wasn't picky about food. It ate everything. Once I even gave it a whole can of sliced pineapple, it disappeared, metal and all. It was like having a giant, alien garbage disposal in the old henhouse. I contemplated what would happen if gave it a computer or a phone but didn't dare after my father had been furious when I dropped my new phone and cracked the screen.

Halloween came and went. I stayed in the henhouse with my homework and didn't dress up. I didn't feel right to trick and treat as a skeleton or ghost with Grandma and all.

"What's on your mind?" the thing asked. "I sense that you are thinking about something difficult."

"Nothing" I lied. "But I do need help with this assignment."

We worked through it. Afterwards, I gave it carrots and corn.

It was completely healed after a couple of weeks. It is amazing what a little old fruit and leftovers can do to an alien. All of the wounds had closed up and left pale, gleaming scars on the smooth surface. Not even the ancient, alien know-it-all could go through life without being ruffled up a bit.

"I am strong enough to leave, this will be our last conversation. Thank you, little mammal."

"I've never been called that before."

"You have treated me well. I will soon depart. You could ask me anything. And I shall answer to the best of my knowledge." I drew a deep breath. I had one question. Actually, the *one* question, the only question that had been burning inside me since Grandma died. A dangerous question that I wasn't sure I wanted an answer to.

"What happens when we die?" There it was, out in the light.

Silence hung between us before it answered.

"We continue."

"Isn't that the opposite of dying? Are you sure you know what you are talking about?"

"Remember, I was there before. I saw the birth of stars. The primal clouds of gas…"

"Jeez, you're worse than Mrs Higgins when she gets going about the Christian church. Just answer the question."

"We continue. Just as you continue. You are a part of the long march."

"I have no idea what you are talking about."

"You are of the universe, as I am of the universe."

"We are nothing alike."

"Neither are you and the plants, or you and a bird. But still, you are the same. Everything in this world, and everything in the universe comes from dying stars. Great white stars glowing strong, and small dying red stars soon to explode. And when they do explode, they spread their matter out in the darkness. And those elements make up everything in the world. From the smallest amoeba to the great whales, and also --you."

"I'm not really sure I understand."

"You are the fabric of stars. Your body is built by atoms and elements that once burned deep in space. Everything in the universe is built from dead stars. And here and now, your body and mind are the continuation of those parts. Long before you, these elements were and when you are dead, the same elements that are in your body will be part of other living things."

"So, Grandma is not really gone?"

"Nothing is ever gone, it just…"

"Continues" I answered.

"See, you have learned. And now it is time for me to leave."

It opened the door and heaved itself out in the night. A gleaming, crawling thing of the stars. It was clumsy on the ground like a giant slug slowly hauling itself over the frozen grass. When it reached the same spot where it had crashed great wings protruded from its body and it rose to the dark sky. It was difficult to single out from the night, its wings calmly keeping it afloat in the air.

"Will I ever see you again?"

"It is unlikely."

And then it was gone. It had returned to the great darkness from where it had come. Slowly I made it back to the house. And stopped, standing in the kitchen. Both Mom and Dad looked up.

"You alright, kid?"

There were not really words for what I felt. But I knew what could make it feel better. I took three cups and placed them on the table. And then one by one, I gathered the ingredients: Cream, sugar, milk and cocoa.

THE END

THE SNAGGLETOOTH WUUF

By Tom Folske

Gilbert "Gravel" Grabowski was a naturally mean kid. He had parents who loved him, and an older sister and younger brother who were pleasant children, but absolutely devised Gravel due to how he treated them. None of that mattered to Gravel though. He was the type of child who would stick used tissues in his sibling's sandwiches before school. He was the kind of kid who broke into his sister's room and stole twenty dollars from her purse, the sort of boy who went into his younger brother's toy box and purposefully broke his favourite toy, then blamed it on the dog.

The dog was a Jack Russell terrier with a lazy eye that Mr. John Grabowski, Gravel's father, fondly named Plissken. The dog was in fact a pup, just under a year old, and had been with the family for about three months now. At first, Gravel had completely ignored the small canine, but one day Plissken had an accident on the carpet at the bottom of the stairs and Gravel stepped in it. The angry, mean-spirited youth began to cuss wildly before walking over and punting the poor dog across the room. Ever since, Gravel had become vengeful and vindictive against the small pup, smacking and kicking it constantly, or doing other malicious things, like throwing garbage in his food bowl or wiping snot on his fur. Even though every single person in the house had scolded him for it, Gravel had continued to harass the poor dog consistently, for the last two months straight.

Plissken wasn't the only animal Gravel abused either, the depraved child tortured all kinds of creatures. He did everything from burning the feet off frogs, to grabbing garter snakes by the tail and whipping them against the ground hard enough to bust their spines in multiple places, to throwing rocks at squirrels and knocking them out of trees. Really, there were too many cruelties to mention in the long and macabre history of animals that ultimately met their untimely ends at the hands of Gilbert "Gravel" Grabowski.

It was a day like any other when Gravel was walking home from school and caught up with his little brother Kent, who was usually way ahead of him, and home several minutes before him. Today, however, Kent was kneeling down by a tree, hunching forward with his face in his jacket.

"What do you think you're doing wuss?"

Kent gasped and jumped, almost falling over. "Nothing," he said, glancing nervously at his older brother before quickly turning around and rushing away. It looked to Gravel as if his younger sibling might have been concealing something in the front of his jacket. Kent may have been quicker on most days, and due to their conflicting body types, Gravel normally wouldn't have been able to catch him on a bad day, but today Gravel caught his little brother by the hood of his jacket and pulled him down backwards, all the way onto his butt.

"What do you got there?" Gravel asked. "You better show me."

"Nothing," Kent said, trying to get up so he could take off running again.

Gravel pulled him right back down, then tackled him onto his side and reached into his jacket to see what he was hiding.

Gravel pulled out a small, orange kitten, which meowed frantically as it was taken away from the warmth and security of Kent's jacket. "You're such a little girl," Gravel said as he grabbed the cat by the tail, and swung it in a circle, causing it to yowl and screech horribly, before he released the helpless animal, sending it flying across a stranger's yard and fortunately into a dense thicket of bushes. The cat got up afterwards, seemingly just scared and not hurt, but it ran away from Kent when he tried to catch it again to soothe it.

"You are a mean person, Gilbert. The Snaggletooth Wuuf will get you. You'll see," Kent cried.

"Shut up baby. How many times do I have to tell you to call me Gravel? Call me Gilbert again and I'm gonna punch you."

"Good. Do it. I don't even care," Kent sobbed. "The Snaggletooth Wuuf is gonna get you and I can't wait." The young boy said coldly before he ran away crying.

Gravel walked slowly back to his house after that, ripping the antenna off a ladybug mailbox, popping a ball some kid had left lying in the yard, and knocking over a couple of trash cans along the way. When he finally did get home, he was expecting to get yelled at by his parents for what he did to Kent's kitten, but instead, he walked through the door, and everything was unnaturally calm.

"Hi Mom, I'm home. I hope there's food," Gravel said, making sure everyone knew he was home.

"There are leftovers in the fridge," his mother called back.

"Hmmm?" Gravel questioned as he went upstairs to see how his brother would retaliate. He rushed to his room first, expecting to find it trashed, ready to give his brother a good beating, but none of his stuff had even been touched.

"What the heck?" Gravel shouted angrily, before stomping over to Kent's room and throwing the door wide open. His little brother was sitting calmly on his bed, smiling, and staring blankly at the wall in front of him. He was holding something in his hand that Gravel couldn't quite make out.

Kent looked toward his older brother and smiled. "I found this on your bed when I went into your room. The Snaggletooth Wuuf left it," the young boy said as he stood up and handed his brother the object he had been holding. It was a palm-sized, crudely made dog bone.

Gravel took one look at the creepy, grotesque bone and dropped it to the ground. "Stop saying that or I'll knock your teeth in."

"I'm not going to say anything," Kent said with a bit too much happiness in his voice like he was in on some secret joke. "Now all I have to do is wait."

Gravel pushed his brother down onto the ground, then left the house just as it started to storm. It was only a light drizzle, and he was wearing a jacket, so he continued walking down the road, ashamed that his little brother had actually started to spook him a little, and looking for something he could take his frustrations out on.

The devious young boy soon came across a small raccoon eating out of a black garbage bag that someone had left at the end of their driveway. Gravel crept up real quietly until he was within throwing distance. He took off his shoe, aimed it perfectly at the hungry critter, and right before he pitched his sneaker, a strange, off-kilter howl reverberated through the night air, causing him to miss the raccoon completely and hit the mailbox next to it. The porch lights of the house at the other end of the driveway flickered on and both the boy and the raccoon scurried away, one of them missing a shoe.

The howl normally wouldn't have bothered Gravel, but all of his little brother's creepiness was really starting to get to him. He was originally going to walk the whole mile down to the grocery store and steal candy from the bins, but now he decided that he was just going to walk the block and a half left to the little store, so he could steal pop instead. First, however, he waited a couple of minutes for things to settle down before going back to retrieve his shoe, and then he continued with his quest in comfort.

"Stupid Snaggletooth Wuuf," Gravel said aloud and to himself, "Can't believe some stupid, ugly-faced, deformed, gross dog is actually getting to me. Screw that. I ain't no girlie-wuss-punk. If I see some dog with a messed-up mouth, I'm gonna punch it."

The young troublemaker started to feel bold again after physically telling off the thing that was making him afraid. He walked up to the little store, then passed it. Gravel was back on course to go to the supermarket. That is until something caught his eye a little way down the dark, narrow alley two blocks beyond the little store.

The startled boy quickly rushed behind a tree so he could get a better look at what he thought he saw without being seen. He peered cautiously through the branches and there, standing in the middle of the alley, was a tall, hooded figure wearing pitch-black robes and carrying a large, sharp-looking scythe. Lightning flashed in the distance and lit up the entire alley for a split second, just enough time for Gravel to get a glimpse of what lay hidden beneath the black hood. There, staring directly at him with something reminiscent of a smile, was the thin, long face of a man-sized dog, complete with one snaggletooth sticking up over its top lip.

Gravel screamed and ran faster than he had run since first grade. He ran full speed all the way back to the little store, where he burst through the door like a lunatic.

"What on Earth is your problem kid?" the cashier asked in confusion.

Gravel put up his index finger in a gesture for her to wait. It took almost three minutes for him to catch his breath enough to speak comfortably and tell his story, but, in that time, he decided against telling them about the cloaked dog thing and instead told them that some crazy old guy chased him down the street with a rake yelling about someone stealing his leaves.

After everyone had calmed down, Gravel asked to use the bathroom before he started back for home. He stole a pop from the cooler and a candy bar on his way out. He enjoyed both moments later, as he leisurely walked home, already starting to forget about the thing he couldn't have seen in the alley.

Gravel was about two blocks away from his house when he heard rustling in the trees across the road. He turned quickly and thought he saw a flash of black, but wasn't certain. The young boy took a few more steps away from that side of the street, quickening his pace a great deal as he did so.

Gravel made it halfway home before the thing in the woods across the road began to growl ferociously. The young boy broke into a run. The thing in the woods ran with him, only now it was barking monstrously, loudly snapping its teeth, and snarling as it went. The sounds were so terrifying that even though he could see his driveway, Gilbert 'Gravel' Grabowski, the self-proclaimed toughest kid in school, peed his pants.

Fortunately for Gravel, he made it all the way home and burst in through the front door.

"Take it easy!" his father shouted from somewhere in the back of the house.

Kent was sitting in the living room watching cartoons. He looked up at his older brother and smiled deviously, though he said nothing.

Gravel glared at his younger sibling fiercely before he marched upstairs to shower and change clothes. When he came back down, Kent was still watching cartoons, and their older sister, Lauren, was sitting beside him.

"Nice trick with the dog costume and the barking," Gravel said bitterly.

"What are you talking about?" Kent replied. "That wasn't me."

"Bull! I know you did it, I just don't know how."

"He has been here watching cartoons since I've been home," Lauren chimed in. "And I saw you leaving as I was pulling up."

"So now you're in on this too?" Gravel asked his sister.

"What are you talking about Gilbert?" Lauren

defended. "You sound like a crazy person."

"Screw this. I'm going to my room," Gravel shouted, stomping upstairs and slamming his bedroom door once he was inside.

"The Snaggletooth Wuuf… That's the stupidest thing I've ever heard of," the irate boy told himself. "Maybe I just haven't been getting enough sleep. I think I will take a nap."

Mrs. Grabowski had made his bed for him and had apparently washed his pillows too because they were on the chair with the still-folded pillowcases sitting on top of them.

"Figures," Gravel mumbled with irritation as he put the pillows back into their cases before throwing them onto the bed. He pulled back the covers, kicked off his shoes, threw his jacket sloppily onto the floor, and crawled cosily into his bed. Gravel immediately found a position that was extremely comfortable, and just about instantly fell asleep. That is until he slid his hand under the pillows he had just thrown down and his fingers made a connection with something small, hard, and undeniably bone-shaped. He pulled the foreign object out from his bedding to reveal another crude dog bone like the one Kent had handed him earlier.

"What the heck is going on?" Gravel angrily asked the empty room, before walking over to his open window and chucking the crudely crafted dog bone into the yard. "This is stupid. There is no such thing as The Snaggletooth Wuuf, and that bone must have been in the pillowcase or something. I'm gonna give Kent a good pounding for this."

Gravel was about to lay back down when the bone he had just thrown popped back in through the window, hitting him square in the back. The young bully turned around to whip the bone at whoever was out there, but when he saw what was standing outside his window, he froze. There, lurking ominously at the furthest edge of his family's backyard, was The Snaggletooth Wuuf, staring straight at him. Gravel screamed, dropped the bone and ran out of his room, all the way back downstairs.

"He's here! He's here!" Gravel screamed as he rushed into the living room.

"What the hell are you talking about," Lauren asked.

Kent just smiled.

Their mother burst into the room. "What on Earth is going on here?" she asked.

"I saw someone in the backyard," Gravel explained.

"I'll go get your father," she replied, disappearing from the room.

A moment later, Mr. Grabowski appeared, and together, Gravel and both of his parents went out to search the backyard.

"Lauren, watch Kent," Mrs Grabowski told her daughter before they went outside.

Gravel and his parents scoured the whole yard, behind trees, in the bushes, and even in the neighbour's yards, but there was no evidence at all that anyone had been out there recently.

"I swear he was here," Gravel almost whined.

"I think maybe you need to cut back on the sweets some," his father told him. "I think you're starting to hallucinate."

"Let's just go back inside," his mother said as his parents proceeded to head into the house.

"I'll be in in a minute," Gravel told them as he visually searched the backyard and surrounding area one more time. "I know you're out there," he whispered angrily.

Gravel looked back, realized he was all alone, and suddenly grew immensely frightened. He started back for his house but didn't make it three steps before he felt a cold, bony paw upon his shoulder. The young bully turned around, beginning to scream just as The Snaggletooth Wuuf latched a collar around his neck. As soon as it tightened, the boy was completely under the beast's control. He couldn't even scream, and when The Snaggletooth Wuuf began to walk, he tugged on the leash extending from the collar and Gravel's body moved as it was commanded.

Fear instantly flooded through Gilbert "Gravel" Grabowski's entire body as The Snaggletooth Wuuf used its large scythe to cut a long, narrow, black hole, right into the middle of the air in the Grabowski family's backyard. Gravel felt like crying, and although he tried desperately to escape, he was all but helpless as the creature disappeared through the gap and pulled him through with it.

The opening closed as soon as they were through, and when Gravel emerged on the other side of the rip, he was both awestruck and terrified. Surrounding him everywhere, in every direction, were animals of all varieties, all standing upright, wearing clothes, and talking with one another at what looked exactly like the flea market that Gravel's father had taken him to when he was younger.

Gravel tried to run, tried to scream, but he still lacked the ability to even struggle as The Snaggletooth Wuuf led him to a large pedestal, one of many, where animal people were already beginning to gather. His captor made Gravel crawl up onto the top of the pedestal and display himself prominently for a large crowd of animal people to gaze upon.

The Snaggletooth Wuuf released his end of the boy's

leash to a cocker spaniel-face attendant, before walking a few steps over to a large podium next to the pedestal.

"Human boy abuses animals, bidding begins at 500 bones," The Snaggletooth Wuuf yelled loudly into the crowd.

"500 bones!" one of the animal people yelled. The owner of the voice was a creature that looked like a mongoose, but the way he acted reminded Gravel of himself, or possibly even worse.

"500 bones going once… twice…sold," The Snaggletooth Wuuf told the mongoose creature.

"Oh, I have such plans for you," the creature deviously told the young human as he was released from the restrictive leash. The boy screamed as the large mongoose creature forced him into an uncomfortable metal cage, in the back of a cramped, awful-smelling carriage, and began to haul him off.

Gravel continued to scream until his new owner reached back and poked him hard in the ribs with a stick and told him to shut up. Gravel began to cry, longing for his family as the mongoose creature looked back at him and smiled.

"You're going to make him into a fine guard human."

THE END

A Deal With The Devil
By Brian MacGowan

"Do you want to make a deal with the devil?"

I looked up from my tablet. Standing at the entrance of my office was the most stunningly beautiful woman I had ever seen. "Wasn't that part of our wedding vows?"

My ex-wife Annette glided into my office like a perfect ballerina and alighted on the edge of my guest chair. "Jeffery, you hurt me so." She leaned forward, "I mean with the real devil."

I cocked one eye, "The devil himself? Lucifer, Beelzebub, the Prince of Darkness, the Lord of the Underworld. That devil?" I leaned back in my chair and shook my head, "Why does it not surprise me that you know him."

"I'm being serious, Jeffery. Do you want to make a deal or not?"

"Why would I want to make a deal with the devil?"

Annette sat back in her chair, "He is a charming fellow, you know."

"I'm sure he is. But once again, why would I want to make a deal? Doesn't he only bargain in souls?" My eyes narrowed. "What did you do?"

"Why must you always be so suspicious?" She fluttered her hands. "But if you must know, he has an option on your eternal soul."

"What do you mean that he has an option on my soul? I don't recall making any form of agreement."

"I might have gotten myself into some trouble. To get myself out, there was a certain agreement — and it involved you."

I closed my eyes and rubbed my head. Annette can be impulsive, which was one of the reasons that I fell in love with her. I thought back to the early part of our relationship when life with Annette was fun and invigorating. All the parties that we went to. All the celebrities were bowled over by her charm and —

I sat bolt upright and stared at her, "Your looks haven't changed one bit since we first met." I moved around the desk and took the seat beside her. "What have you done?"

Her hands started to tremble. She reached into her purse, pulled out her compact, opened it and stared at its mirror. She handed it to me. "Look into it, what do you see?"

I tentatively held it and looked into the mirror. Moving my head, I looked at both of my profiles. I looked back at Annette, "What am I supposed to see? It is just me."

"That's right, it's you. What you look like. What you *really* look like." She took the thing from my hand and shifted in her seat so we would both be in the compact mirror. "Now, what do you see?"

Looking back at me was Annette but with a disfigured visage. A savage scar ran across her face, her left eye white with blindness. I gently held her hand and closed the compact mirror. Still holding her hand, I turned her toward me. "I don't understand."

"Before we met, I was in a horrible car accident. My friend Amber and I were out bar hopping. I was driving and..." She trailed off, lost in the past. "You know those deals you make when you are desperate. You usually make them to God, but God wasn't listening. So, I changed it, and the devil listened. I wanted the accident to have never happened. I wanted Amber to live and for me to be beautiful again. But it doesn't work that way. The devil can't change the past. He can only affect the present. So, he made me beautiful again. But my punishment is that I see my true self every time I look into the compact."

"So, how do I come in? Why must I make a deal with the devil?"

"To maintain my looks, I must give the devil a soul every five years."

"I still don't understand." She handed me a legal

document. I looked at it. "Our divorce decree?"

Annette shrugged and winced, "I was mad at you at the time. I knew that you wouldn't fully read the settlement. You agreed to give up certain assets, both material as well as the embodiment of immaterial assets. I wanted to damn you to Hell."

I stood up quickly, "Well, apparently you succeeded." I paced the room, my head feeling like it was about to explode. "How could you! You had no right!"

"I know. But at the time, I wanted to kill you for what you did to me."

I spun around and glared at her, "Me? You're the one who..." I stopped, closed my eyes, and took a deep breath. "Look, we've been through this already." I sat in my office chair. "What deal do I have to make to get my soul back?"

"You need to acquire something. Something that the devil desires but cannot obtain himself."

"So, what is this something that I need to acquire? And why can't the Almighty Prince of Darkness do it himself? It kind of ruins his street cred if he needs someone else to do his dirty work."

"You need to find Thomas Jefferson's Cremona violin. When you do, contact me. I will make the arrangements after that." She rose and headed to the door.

"Where am I supposed to find this violin?"

Annette stopped and turned, "You're the detective... detect."

After Annette left, I stared at the door, trying to make sense of it all. I knew she had hired a good divorce lawyer, but I didn't think she would get the Master Manipulator himself. Somehow, to regain my soul, I need to acquire this Jefferson violin. Acquire! Right, she meant to steal it. This is not something that you find online. Click add to cart and wait two days for delivery. If I can't buy it online, I should at least, be able to find it online.

I picked up my tablet and plugged in the search terms. One of the first hits was my target violin. Figures, it is in Jefferson's Monticello estate in Virginia. That is not something that they will have in the gift shop. I clicked on the link about his violins. Well, I'll be. His violins are currently in a travelling exhibit. And they are just two hours from here.

Mid-morning the next day, I showed up at the exhibit of Thomas Jefferson's life. I took a lingering tour of the exhibit, not wanting to look too eager. I finally made my way to the Music of Jefferson section. The violin was beautiful, but to me, it looked like any other violin. I tried to surreptitiously figure out what type of security they might have on the violin. Nothing was obvious to me. They appeared to rely more on building security than securing the actual artefacts. I strolled around the exhibit, observing the security measures. I made my way back to my prey.

I studied the violin and its setting, trying to figure out how to get it out of the building. A woman came up beside me. "Beautiful, isn't it?"

I ignored her.

"They say that this is his most famous musical instrument. There are a lot of people, powerful entities, who are desperate to acquire it."

I inwardly cringed. I have been found out. She is probably part of their security task force, specifically looking for someone wanting to do a quick snatch-and-grab. I turned to her. "I'm just looking. I don't even play the violin." I turned and left the exhibit.

Exiting the building, I stopped at the bottom of the steps. I shouldn't hang around and attract more attention, but I need more information. I started to casually walk away. I'll grab a bite to eat, head back before closing, and stake out their lock-up procedures.

The exhibit closed at eight o'clock, and I watched from the coffee shop across the street, sipping my coffee. The woman from earlier that day sat down next to me.

"You know, the only thing that this will tell you is

when they lock the front door. You have no idea what happens on the inside. Sure, you saw the equipment that they wanted you to see. But what about the other security measures, the hidden ones?"

I didn't even look her way, "Listen, I'm not wanting any trouble. I'm just drinking my coffee and looking out of the window."

"Really, because it seems like you're staking the place out to me. You're trying to figure out how to steal the Cremona violin."

I kept looking out the window, "I don't know who you are, and you certainly don't know me. Just leave me alone and let me enjoy my coffee."

"Jeffery, is that right? Can I call you Jeff," I stared hard at her. "Right, Jeffery, it is. Why don't we go down the street to the bar? I'll tell you what I know about the violin. We will part ways if you don't believe me or aren't interested. You'll never see me again. I'll even buy the first round."

"I'm comfortable here."

"It's not safe here. We're not protected. It must be at the bar or not at all."

"Then I guess it is not at all. I would say, 'See you around,' but I don't want to see you again."

"I can see that you don't trust me, and I don't blame you. I'll be down the street. If you should change your mind, come on down."

I continued looking out the window, but I didn't see anything. My mind was chewing on this latest conversation. She was right. All I know is when they lock the door. Not one guard or staff member has come out through the main gates, meaning there must be another entrance. I took a swig of coffee. Ugh, it was cold. I looked at the bottom of my cup, "Ah, what the Hell. If I'm going to drink something cold, it might as well be a beer."

I left the coffee shop. A neon sign caught my eye two blocks away, to my left. I shoved my hands in my pockets and strolled down the street. The Rock and the Rooster came into view. I entered the pub, which was designed like a traditional English pub. I searched for the woman. The bartender nonchalantly motioned to a booth in the corner. My *friend* was seated with her back to the door, two dark stouts sitting untouched on the table.

I sat heavily on the other side of the table. She pushed one of the beers across the table toward me. "First off, let me introduce myself. My name is Samantha Adams, but you can call me..."

"Sam?"

"Sam. My father was a historian and a demon hunter."

I laughed, "A demon hunter."

"Says the man who is trying to buy his soul back from the devil."

I raised my beer glass. Point to Sami.

"Satan has your soul, but you must give him Thomas Jefferson's Cremona violin to get it back. But you have no idea how to get it. Is that about it?"

I took a swallow of beer, "How do you know so much about this?"

"The actions of Annette Taylor are not unknown to us. We figured that she would be contacting you sooner or later. We just didn't know exactly what she needed you to acquire. It became obvious to us when you showed up today at the Jefferson exhibit."

I leaned forward, "Who is this *us* that you have been referring to? Are you federal?"

Sami also leaned forward, "I am not at liberty to say who we are but suffice to say there is more at risk than just your soul."

"No offence, I'm just concerned about my soul. The rest is your business. Now, how can we steal that violin?"

"Aren't you the least bit curious why the devil would want a violin?"

"Not particularly. What the devil does is his own business."

Sami gave me a stern look, "What the devil does is everybody's business."

I swung my beer glass in a grand theatrical arc, "Please enlighten me."

"Do you know the Charlie Daniels Band song 'The Devil Went Down to Georgia?'"

"Sure"

"What if I said that the song was not all that far off from the truth."

I gave her a cock-eyed glance, "So you are saying that the devil actually went down to Georgia and challenged Johnny to a violin duel."

"Not fully. It is more like he went down to Virginia and challenged Thomas Jefferson."

I covered a smile with my hand, "So Thomas Jefferson, the guy who wrote the Declaration of Independence, a Founding Father and former president, challenged the devil to a violin contest. I suppose Jefferson won."

"Well, he didn't challenge the devil. It was actually the devil that challenged Jefferson. As you may know, Thomas Jefferson was an accomplished violinist who owned at least three violins. The most famous is the Cremona, which is the violin that Jefferson played. But basically, yeah, Jefferson won. Enraged by the loss, in 1770, the devil sought to destroy the violin by burning

Shadwell plantation, Jefferson's home at that time. The farmstead burned to the ground, but the violin survived."

"So why did the devil challenge Jefferson?"

Sami thought for a moment, "There has always been good and evil in the world. The balance flows back and forth, but generally, they equal each other out. The American colonies were pushing back evil. War was coming. Everyone knew that. They just didn't know when. The devil was looking for the upper hand. He wanted free reign during the conflict. Jefferson, Adams, Franklin, and Washington stood in his way. He challenged them to pick a champion. They would duel for supremacy. The loser would not interfere in the upcoming war. The four, who would become part of our Founding Fathers, agreed on one condition. That they would choose the weapon."

"They chose a violin? Poor weapon choice."

"That's what the devil thought. But what he did not know was that the Cremona violin was strung using some of the guts of the devil himself."

I put up my hands, "Hold it! The violin was strung using his own intestines? How would he not know this?"

"He has fought many battles under many different names. Sometimes, he wins. Sometimes, he loses. In one such battle with the Babylonians, he was gravely wounded with a spear to the abdomen, spilling a part of his guts on the battlefield. The Babylonians retrieved his entrails, dried them and used them to string musical instruments. The music from these instruments can be used to conquer the devil. Over the millennia, many of these instruments have been lost or destroyed. Only four strings have survived; those are on Jefferson's Cremona violin."

I moved to the other side of the booth, sitting next to Sami. "That explains why they chose the violin. But how did Jefferson know about the strings?"

"Jefferson knew about the strings through Benjamin Franklin, who got them from the French crown. King Louis did not want the English to win in the Americas. Eventually, the devil learned of the French deception, and we all know what happened to their aristocracy."

I became enthralled with the story. "So Jefferson strung his violin using the devil's guts and won the challenge. But after all this time, why does the devil want the violin, and why can't he get it himself?

Sami looked up at the talking heads on the television. "Evil is constantly stalking the world. Recently, it is getting stronger. The devil has never forgotten about being defeated by Jefferson. That violin can stand in his way. He needs it destroyed."

"But that doesn't explain why he can't do it himself."

"The bridge of the violin is a talisman. The devil and other demons cannot touch the violin as long as the talisman is intact."

"You are going to help me steal the violin so he can destroy it, and I get my soul back." I sat back, taking a long swig of beer. Sami didn't say anything.

"No. You cannot allow the violin to be destroyed," I concluded. "So, why are you wasting my time?"

She turned to me, "You are correct. We can't allow the violin to be damaged. We already have demon-gut strings, just not from the devil himself. We plan to steal the violin and shave off just enough of the strings to imbue the demon-gut strings with the devil's essence. We will then put them onto a matching Cremona violin."

"What about the talisman?"

Sami waved her hand. "For us, talismans like that are relatively easy to come by. The devil won't know the difference.

"What if he does notice? You are playing with my soul here."

"Trust us, we have done similar operations. He won't notice a thing."

I felt uneasy. "So what's the next step? When do we steal the violin."

Sami got up from the table and then turned toward me. "The next step is all ours. You are not involved. There is an orchestral strings convention at the Cranmore Hotel in three days. The police won't notice an extra violin case. Meet me there in the lobby, five o'clock sharp."

A day later, the Thomas Jefferson exhibit closed prematurely. The news outlets were reporting that an undisclosed artefact was missing. Two days after that, I made my way to the Cranmore Hotel. I was trying to wait patiently in the lobby when I heard my name announced. I approached the concierge desk, identifying myself. Apparently, they located my misplaced violin.

Upon returning to my office, Annette was already there, awaiting me. She rushed toward me, exclaiming, "Do you have it? Let me see it." I reached for the clasps on the case, but she stopped me, saying, "No, no. It is best that I do not see it. Just give me the case. Meet me at midnight tomorrow at the old cannery, dock six." She grabbed the case and headed for the door. She stopped and turned, saying, "Wait, we need to prepare. Make it eleven-thirty."

Having been literally sold to the devil by Annette, I really had no trust in her. The next day, I staked out dock six. There was no activity until about ten o'clock that night. Annette pulled up to the loading dock, offloading several boxes. When I felt she was not coming back outside, I made my way to the dock. Carefully, I opened the door and snuck in, keeping to the shadows. In the middle of the loading area, she had drawn a pentagram. She stood naked in the centre, mumbling what sounded like ramblings. I could make out a pattern to the rambling, with each successful iteration becoming louder. Finally, at a full shout, the pentagram started to glow. Fires grew from the outside lines moving to the centre. The heat from the fires was intense, the smell of brimstone overwhelming. A large horned beast materialised in the centre portion—the devil himself. I was disappointed not to see him holding a pitchfork. I shrank further into the shadows."

The devil looked down at Annette. He bent low toward her, sniffing the air around her. "Why have you brought me here?"

"Master, I have Jefferson's Cremona violin." She moved toward the violin, picking up the case and offering it to the devil.

The devil regarded Annette, "The deal was for your man's soul. Are you changing it?"

"Yes, Master, I want to exchange the Cremona violin for my eternal beauty."

"But you already have eternal beauty."

"Yes, Master, But I want to be whole and not just a mirage of my former self."

Emerging from my hiding spot, the devil's eyes darted toward me. He sniffed the air once more. "There is another here. Step out, mortal." With a wave, he extinguished the pentagram fire, leaving the area illuminated solely by the glow of the pentagram burned into the floor.

I approached the outer ring, the heat still radiating from it. The devil stepped closer, his nostrils flaring and then licking his lips. "You are one of mine. I own you." He looked toward Annette. "He is your man." He looked back at me. "Why are you here, mortal?"

She tricked me, and my efforts over the last few days were for nought because of her deception. She had no plans to return my soul; it was all a ruse. She used me for her own vain desires. But she didn't know that she wasn't holding the real Cremona violin.

"I am here to bear witness, Oh Great One."

"Witness? Witness to what?"

Annette stepped forward, "That's right, Master, he is here to witness your greatest triumph when you destroy this accursed violin."

The devil stood up, "Who brings this tribute to me?"

Annette kneeled, holding the violin case high, "I do, Master."

Eager to see the violin, the devil rubbed his hands together. "Open the case so I can examine it."

"Yes, Master."

The devil reached out, hovering his hand over the violin but not touching it. He did it again, but slower. He sniffed the air and licked his lips. He bent low and examined the violin. "What trickery is this?"

Annette stammered, "N-n-none Master." She glanced over at me, worried.

"It is your testimony that this is the true Cremona violin?"

"Y-y-yes Master."

The devil snatched the violin from Annette, "This is *not* the Cremona violin," he roared, crushing the instrument into pieces. He towered over her, and she trembled in fear. He reached down and violently lifted her from the floor, bringing her face to face with his own. "You have deceived me!"

She tried to speak, his grip constricting her lungs. All she could manage was a "M-m-m." A fiery hole appeared in the centre of the pentagram. Screams and moans of the damned emanated from the pit below. He raised her above his head, then thrust her deep down into damnation.

He withdrew his empty hand, and the hole slowly sealed. He turned to face me, his eyes narrowing.

Stepping to the outer ring, he bent low and looked me in the eye.

"Do you want to make a deal with the devil?"

THE END

DON'T CROSS MOTHER
By Lady Lyndsey Holloway

The wind carried the smell of the dust kicked into the air by the recent rains. Earthy and clean all in the same breath.

Agatha stumbled down the uneven, rocky path that led towards the cave nestled along the river's edge, one hand upon her engorged stomach, the other on the steep stone wall to keep her balance.

She cried out as another contraction twisted her belly and pain ricocheted through every fibre of her being, her knees nearly buckling. Gritting her teeth against the agony, Agatha clung to the rocks, her nails shattered with the effort to keep her upright.

"Not too far now. One more corner, past the pool, and then shelter. Away from prying eyes." She thought, breathing deeply as she forced her feet to move, her hand guiding her path in the dying light.

The wind whipped at her, snatching at the scarf that covered her head and face, threatening to steal it from her entirely if she didn't reach the caves soon. Thunder cracked overhead, and Agatha turned her face to the black clouds, cursing them under her breath as the first huge droplets of rain slapped her in the face.

"You could not have waited a moment more?! The path is treacherous enough already, let alone sodden!" She hissed at them.

No such luck, not for her, not in her life. Alone, without anyone to support her, as was the lot of many a young girl in this world. No matter, her daughter would have a better life, she would grow up stronger, Agatha had seen to that.

She swallowed hard while the storm screamed above. She took each step carefully, moving as quickly as she dared. It wasn't far, she could see the flat path that led alongside the skull-shaped pool beneath the mossy ledge. Just beyond that lay the small cave she'd scouted as a good place to have her baby. The townsfolk wouldn't offer her shelter, not an orphan like her. *Especially* if they knew who had fathered her child. She hadn't *known* it was *him*, not when he'd courted her, not until *after* the affair, but he'd promised her daughter would do great things, and she believed him.

Lightning flashed across the sky and lit the way as she shuffled past the pool. She'd enjoyed listening to the steady drip of water drop from the mossy ledge above splashing into the mirror-like surface of the water. But today the rain beat it like a drum, huge droplets tore into the surface and flooded over the lichen-covered rocks onto her bare feet.

Agatha shivered and another contraction caught her off guard. This time she had nothing to steady herself, and the pain was too much to bear. Gasping, she collapsed to her knees with a wail. She barely felt the rock tear into her knees, it could not *remotely* compare to the fire in her stomach.

The baby was coming, and she was coming *now*.

"Just a little further." Agatha whimpered, dragging herself along the slippery rocks to the dark maw of the cave.

Lightning ripped the sky in two and showed Agatha her salvation. With one last pull, she pulled herself over the steep stone lip and rolled down the sloping floor to a natural wallow under the caves' jagged roof. The floor was almost oddly smooth, as though someone had come and carved it to be as comfortable as possible while leaving the natural rock above as a reminder of the teeth the earth once had here.

Whimpering, Agatha shuffled to the back of the cave and leaned against the wall, panting as she found a comfortable position. She placed her hands on her swollen belly and felt the baby shift.

It was time.

The roar of thunder drowned out Agatha's agonised screams, as though she and the storm raged as one, until at last her pain ended with a sigh of relief. Sobbing, she pulled the scarf from her head and wrapped it around the babe lying on the cave floor. Agatha wiped the tears from her eyes and gasped at the sight of her daughter, and a buzzing filled her ears.

What stared back was not the beautiful little girl she'd imagined since his promise of a strong daughter. Instead, the baby had a large, crooked nose, hunched back, and crooked legs. Mother and daughter met one another's eyes as the thunder cracked overhead. Agatha expected her daughter to start crying, instead, she cackled and the storms that had raged during her birth ceased entirely.

***

"Where is Ursula?"

"Ursula! *Ursula!*"

The sound of her foster family calling for her made Ursula smile. They were some of the few who accepted her as she was – a deformed young woman with no evidence of which lineage she belonged to, only the rumours that flittered about regarding her birth – but even they were suspicious of her.

Too like her birth mother, that's what she'd heard them say behind closed doors when they weren't aware she was lurking in the shadows. Too comfortable in the Forest of Knaresborough for the liking of the townsfolk, but they couldn't deny her talents. Once too often her remedies cured what ailed folk, and problems were often solved once brought to her attention.

Hadn't she retrieved Mrs Miller's brand-new smock and petticoat after they'd been stolen? Hadn't she and Joan stood at the Market Cross when Agnes Ambler danced and skipped her way to them, singing all the way – "I stole my neighbour's smock and coat, I am a thief and here I show it!" – the missing items in hand. Joan had watched Agnes with a mixture of shock and fear while the woman handed the offending clothing to the waiting Ursula, curtsied, and skipped away still singing. It hadn't been fear of Agnes, the woman was harmless, albeit light-fingered; but Ursula was another matter entirely. It hadn't bothered Ursula when her neighbour trembled as she took back the missing items, nor when Joan hurried away with several furtive glances in her direction. Ursula had helped when asked, and that was all that mattered.

"Ursula?!" Her mother called again in a panicked tone.

Ursula chuckled, that meant someone *important* was looking for her.

"Toby, she only listens to you." Her foster father

sighed, but it was the name that made Ursula's heart dance and her smile soften.

She'd always been a mischievous child; apt to wander off if left unattended, and not afraid of anything. Her foster mother enjoyed telling tales of her many 'adventures', most of which involved Ursula scaring the ever-living bejeesus out of those around her, only 'confirming' their suspicions that her father was… well… they didn't like to say *his* name aloud. Her impish streak didn't dissipate with age. Her love for the Forest and dancing in the rain grew as she did. Only one person could calm the fire in her heart.

Tobias Shipton. Her Toby.

"Mother Shipton," he called, using the nickname he'd coined upon their marriage, "my love, you're required at home," his soft voice carried upon the wind, through the trees, to where Ursula hid in the branches of a tall oak.

She'd snuck away in the early morning to gather herbs and plants for her potions. She had a small community of regulars who paid good coin for her tinctures. Simple vials that made stiffened hands release their death-like grip enough for the taker to feel relief and be able to harvest for another year. Plenty feared her, more suspected her, but Toby loved her. Despite what *many* townsfolk might whisper about their marriages, Toby loved her for who she was, and Ursula never hid her nature from him. He'd seen her in the woods as a child and been fascinated by her; he was the only one who'd seen *beyond* her deformities to the woman that lurked within the haggard, hunched frame. She knew even her foster family, while accepting of her appearance and 'slightly' unusual ways, wondered why the handsome carpenter had asked for her hand in marriage.

Slipping from the branch, she alighted upon the leaf-strewn ground with an elegance she shouldn't have been party to. She picked up her walking staff and limped her way through the undergrowth, her back bowed as ever, leaving the question as to *how* she'd got into the tree a mystery to all but the oak and the wind that whistled through the autumn leaves.

"I take it someone calls for me?" She asked as she neared the edge of the forest, reluctant to step out into exposure, the Forest embraced her as she was and made her whole. It was home.

"They do, my love, and even *I* cannot turn them away. Not this time." Toby smiled as he bridged the gap between them, bending to kiss her cheek lovingly.

Her breath caught in her throat and a tingle ran along her crooked spine as always when he touched her. He was a good man, simple in some ways compared to others, but genuine and kind, and he loved her beyond what words could ever say. Good with his hands, he'd carved their home to suit her needs, making chairs, tables, and utensils to ease the pain her deformities caused.

"Oh?" Ursula straightened her back as best she could, using her staff as she raised an eyebrow questioningly at her husband, before glancing at her foster family, all of whom stared at her.

There was an air of terrified excitement amongst them that she couldn't attribute to her, for once, and a sound in the back of Ursula's mind – like the flapping of a moth's wings – warned her that trouble could be on the horizon. Whoever had come must have gone to her family to look for her, first and foremost, since her marriage was still new, and it was doubtful that news had spread much further than the borders of Knaresborough itself.

"The Mayor of York wishes to see you, love." Toby smiled.

"Does he now?" Ursula replied with a wry smile.

She knew the Lord Mayor, not personally, but by reputation at least. Words of her talents had spread, even if news of her marriage hadn't. People came from far and wide to see her, either to cure some ailment or other or to find out their future. She did not doubt that the Lord Mayor was of the latter since he'd made his opinion of her *quite* clear over the years. He disliked her, to put it mildly, in truth he feared her. He, like so many others, liked to throw the word 'Witch' around when discussing her. While Ursula had never disagreed with that label, neither had she agreed to it.

Toby gave her a small smile, and she grinned back, wholly aware that her foster family watched them uneasily. They'd never been comfortable with her predictions, nor with the ease, she dished them out to the dignitaries that dared cross their threshold to obtain them from the daughter they'd taken in. She gave her mother a small, apologetic smile and looked up at her husband.

"I suppose I'd best not keep him waiting any longer then."

"Perhaps not." He chuckled, taking her elbow, leaving the other arm free to use her staff to support herself.

"Ursula." Her mother called softly, the unease plain in her tone.

Ursula turned to look at the woman, eyebrow raised questioningly.

"Just - just be careful." The woman added in a quiet voice as if she couldn't quite find the words, she wanted to convey how she *really* felt.

Ursula nodded, at least *acknowledging* what the woman said, even if nothing would change her attitude.

The walk back to the humble house she shared with Toby was long, considering every step took all the mental fortitude she had. It amused her, in a way, that so many came to *her* for their ailments, yet never questioned why she hadn't fixed her own. They loved to bandy the word 'Witch' around in fear of her talents, but the moment she was useful they bit their tongues and came crawling to her on their knees, coin in hand.

She was the Devil's Daughter when it suited them, but Ursula was accustomed to their prejudices. It only fuelled her need for solitude. There *was* no cure for her deformities, 'magic' or otherwise. She'd been born this way; she would die this way. Even *if* the Devil *was* her father, he'd been absent from her life, like many illegitimate fathers tended to be. She expected no favours, even from him.

Toby led her along the cobbled streets to their house by the river. She'd wanted to be as close to the Forest as possible, and their house allowed her husband to have a workshop to complete the commissions he received. The rest of the townsfolk preferred her out of the way; close enough to visit when they needed to, but not *too* close that they feared falling under a curse. She could make her way up the hill to the Market Cross and main square, but she preferred to stay by the river if she could.

As they rounded the corner, it was hard to miss the crowd gathered around their thatched cottage. The townsfolk had clearly heard she had a visitor of renown, otherwise, they wouldn't have come in such great numbers to linger outside her door. Ursula snorted and glanced at Toby as she felt his hand squeeze her elbow. She sighed softly and nodded. He let her go and strode on ahead to part the mob so she could walk through them more easily. Chances were they would have scattered once they realised she was there, but Toby's first thought was *always* of her. Which probably made their assumptions that she'd bewitched him only more real in their minds.

Standing beside her door was a pompous-looking man wearing a thick velvet coat of deepest burgundy, the cuffs puffed at his upper arms to expose the elaborately handwoven lace sleeves that graced his wrists. The simple linen wool hose he wore ended in brightly polished leather shoes; expensive and far less comfortable than the simple leather she wore.

The many jewelled rings that adorned his fingers glistened in the sun, along with the Mayoral medal he wore around his neck, carrying York's insignia. Even *without* the costume jewellery, she would have known who he was, given the air of snobbery that *wafted* off him like the stench of pig dung off a farmer. Then again, there wasn't *much* difference between dignitaries and pig dung as far as Ursula was concerned.

His beady brown eyes turned her way, and he narrowed his gaze at her suspiciously. He'd come to her for a prophecy, no doubt hoping to hear of some glorious future he thought he deserved, despite his feelings towards her. Hatred, he *hated* what she was, and hated himself *more* because he needed her. The irony.

"Mrs Shipton?" He asked as she made her way down the slope.

"Correct, and you would be the Lord Mayor of York? To what do I owe such an honour?" She smiled, ignoring the soft sigh from Toby that served as exasperation and a warning against pushing her luck.

"I am. Your reputation precedes you, madam, I seek your counsel and your prophecies." The mayor replied in an aloof tone, nose turned upwards as he looked down the length of it at her.

She glanced at her husband out of the corner of her eye as he shuffled nervously beside their door. Ursula nodded to the Lord Mayor and motioned for the man to enter their humble abode while Toby held the door open for them. The mayor went in first and Toby helped

Ursula over the threshold before he closed out the rest of the world.

"Please, follow me, sir." Ursula placed her staff beside the door and shuffled her way through the house, using the walls for support as she made her way to the dining table, nestled at the back of the house where she could look out over the river.

Ursula settled onto the seat closest to the window, brushing against the curtains that kept out the worst of the cold in the winter, sending an eclipse of moths into the air. The mayor sneered, his lip curled in disgust as the insects fluttered and flew about his head, sending a cascade of glittering wing dust over his face before they returned to the rafters and the safety of the darkness.

"Now, I must warn you, sir, that you may not like what the future holds." Ursula clasped her hands together, watching the mayor carefully as he manoeuvred his bulky clothing in the seat opposite her.

He snorted as he brushed at the remnants of crumbs from their simple breakfast of bread and gruel. "Just make your predictions, *Witch*, I shall deal with the rest."

Wings fluttered overhead as the moths shifted uneasily at his tone. A cacophony of hissing, delicate appendages flapped in unison. Ursula tapped a finger on the table and the sound hushed, the moths quieted by her calm aura despite the man's clear insult. She opened her palms to the ceiling, and two of the moths alighted upon them, opening, and closing their wings steadily as she smiled at them.

"And you're *sure* you wish to know?" Ursula asked, her eyes never leaving the insects cradled in her hands.

"Yes, yes! Get *on* with it." The mayor hissed as he shifted irritably in his seat.

Ursula glanced at him for a moment from under her eyelashes before she closed her eyes and focused on the moths in her hands. She could feel their tiny claws hook into her skin, their abdomens soft and furry, their delicate wings like silk against her calloused skin.

She breathed slowly and whispered softly, "When there is a Lord Mayor living in Minsteryard, let him beware of a stab." Her voice almost echoed through the room, as if drawn from beyond the world they knew.

"What nonsense is this?!" The mayor hissed.

"Nonsense, sir?" Ursula cooed, opening her eyes to meet his angry gaze as he slammed his fists onto the table, knocking over the chair in his haste to stand.

"Are you threatening me, madam?"

"No, sir, *I* am not. I merely catch glimpses of the future; it was *you* who came to *me*. I warned you that you might not like what I had to say."

"You are a *fraud*, a cripple who preys upon the weak-minded. Devil's Daughter indeed, only one spawned by *Satan* would spew such falsities!" He spat at her as he hurried away from the table, giving her another nervous look over his shoulder as he threw open her front door and hurried outside, slamming it behind him.

Dust rained from the ceiling and the moths flapped their wings violently, filling the house with a hurricane of movement while the mayor shouted and screamed outside about the witch threatening his life.

"Ursula." Toby sighed as he peered into the street.

"I told him only what was there. And given his attitude it was *hardly* a taxing prophecy. If this is how he behaves with his constituents, it's only a matter of time before *one* of them stabs him." Ursula retorted as she gently shook the moths from her hands and gave her husband an apologetic smile. "I wish I could say I did it purely to annoy him, unfortunately, his fate was sealed *long* before he chose to hear it."

Toby sighed again and strode over to kiss her forehead. "You'll get into trouble one of these days, my love."

"I'm not afraid of them, I'll be fine."

"I hope so, for *both* our sakes." Toby chuckled.

***

Thunder boomed and drowned out her screams as the

ice-cold raindrops mingled with the tears on her face.

He was gone. Her beloved Toby was gone.

She'd returned from the Forest, her basket laden with herbs and plants. Ordinarily, her husband would come to fetch her home, since she tended to lose track of time when left to her own devices, away from the prying and judgemental eyes of the townsfolk. It'd been strange walking home alone, even more so when she'd called his name and silence answered.

Ursula collapsed to her knees, her fingers left deep gouges in the mud and leaf detritus as she remembered the terrible emptiness that filled her home once she was inside. There was no sign of her beloved, no indication he was there. For one moment, she wondered if madness had set in, and their married life had been a dream. The moths had led her to where he lay; gathering en masse at the door to his workshop, the soft hush of their flapping filled the silence of their house and her stomach as it churned.

She hadn't wanted to open the door, she'd been afraid of what lay beyond it, and reality had been no better than the fantasy built in her mind. The unearthly wail that left her throat at the sight of Toby's body heaped on the floor had been foreign even to her. No matter how she shook him, or what techniques or potions she tried, she could not rouse him from his eternal slumber, yet it struck her that he didn't seem at peace. The twisted expression lingering on his face as she cradled his head in her lap would haunt her for all eternity, and she'd left her heart with him as she stumbled from the workshop.

Her cries had been heard, and she vaguely recalled someone brushing past her as she staggered into the kitchen and gripped the table, trying to catch her breath.

"He's dead! Tobias is dead!"

"*She* did it, that *witch*."

"Remember what she said to the Lord Mayor? She *said* he'd be stabbed if he lived in Minsteryard, and he did, he got stabbed and died!"

The voices mingled into one, she was sure she knew who they belonged to, but she couldn't *think* above the endless frantic flapping of the moths in her head. Someone put a hand on her shoulder, but she brushed them off and hurried from the house she'd shared with the only man she would ever live with. Instinctively she grabbed the staff Toby carved her and pushed her way through the crowd outside her house as the storm broke above.

The Forest waited to embrace her, as it always did, and she released her grief into the storm, safely away from the townsfolk. As if *she* would kill her Toby? Then again, they'd always believed she'd enchanted him to marry her in the first place. They'd never understood how any man could *actually* love her the way that he had.

And now he was gone.

The wind caressed her cheek gently, despite the storm that raged around her. It encouraged her to stand, to push on a little longer. She knew where to go, where she would call home from now on. It was somewhere she should never have left, the place of her birth. Guided by the cold hand of the wind, and embraced by the shivering rain, Ursula limped and shuffled through the mud and leaves to the stone path that led to the river's edge. Ordinarily, she would have feared tumbling down the wet rocks and snapping her neck, but she feared no such thing now. Only Death would reunite her with Toby, she might not take her own life, but she welcomed whatever fate awaited her.

As she ducked beneath the overhanging rock and took shelter at the edge of the pool, the storm calmed. She stared at her reflection in the water and sneered at the hook-nosed face that looked back at her with its hunched shoulders. There was a steady '*plink, plink, plink*' as the rainwater dripped from the overhanging vegetation, not green as it should be but stiff and grey as if made from stone. She smiled slightly, though there was no warmth to the expression.

Ursula knew the secrets of this place, she'd learnt

them a long time ago, though she'd kept it from even Toby. He might have loved her, warts and all, but she didn't want him to fear her true power. It didn't matter now, did it? He was gone, and the town believed *she'd* done it. The storm roared to life above her, but she remained dry in her little part of the world. Something drew her attention to the Forest above, and she saw the flickering orange torchlights and knew that some of the men had come to find her. Their belief that she'd murdered her husband fuelled their courage to confront her, no doubt.

Using her staff, she stood and limped towards the cave where her mother had given birth to her in a storm such as this. Standing in the entrance, staff clasped in both hands before her, she turned to face the men who'd come to do her harm. They were lucky that Toby's death had been so recent, his influence over her remained and she silently promised to do no more than frighten them. She still needed them, and as much as they feared and probably hated her, they needed her.

"Ursula Shipton!" One man called out, and she recognised the voice of Thomas Miller, husband of Joan, who she'd retrieved the clothing for two years hence.

"*Mother* Shipton," she retorted, her tone firm and strong even as her heart shattered at the use of the name her beloved had gifted her.

"You are no *mother* unless you nurture the Devil's babes at your breast!" Another voice hissed.

"No. I am no mother, not in the sense that your wife is, John Marten, but have I not been Mother to this town as and when it pleased you?" She replied calmly, even as her fingers gripped her staff tightly. She and Toby had been happy together, but the townsfolk had often pointed out their lack of offspring, muttering that it was unlikely the Devil's Daughter could conceive naturally. "Did I not save your boy when he was ill? Or have you chosen to forget my kindness?"

"We cannot forget the good you have done, *Mother* Shipton. But your husband is dead, and your prophecy about the mayor was true. So many of the things you've said have come true, you must see the sense of it." Thomas Miller called, wincing as the thunder clapped overhead as if *it* answered for her.

"The sense of *what*? That you believe I murdered my husband?" She hissed, unable to keep the anger from her tone this time. "I will give you one warning. Leave me in peace and only return *here* in a similar mindset, or I *shall* make you regret it."

"Kill the witch!" Marten cried as he rushed towards her, axe held aloft, torch in his other hand as he skirted around the edge of the pool, slipping and sliding on the wet rock as he aimed to finish her where she stood.

"I'm sorry, my darling, I cannot stand by and do nothing. I won't hurt them… well… I won't kill them, but I will give them a good scare." She thought as she tightened her grip and drew herself as straight as she could.

The storm fell silent, and flames flickered to life behind her, summoned from the depths of a realm none of the men wanted to believe existed. The shadows formed a shape over her shoulder. Mother Shipton caught a glimpse of the horned creature cast from the fire out of the corner of her eye. There was nothing there, not really, little more than a reminder of who her father was *supposed* to be, though the Devil was too busy to show himself, let alone help her. Not that she needed *him*, not when she had her friends.

Something caused the flames to shudder and shift, dispelling the image of the horned man and his cloven feet, leaving only darkness. Marten gasped, sliding to a halt, and losing his footing, collapsing at her feet with Miller and the other men a step behind. The storm still raged above, but the only sound they could hear was the incessant flutter of *wings*. Mother Shipton smiled, and the flames that had sprung to life behind her vanished as the air stirred into a vortex. It *moved* behind her, a living mass of bodies and fragile wings as the moths surrounded and shrouded her body with their own.

"*Run!*" Miller snapped at Marten, shoving his hands under the man's arms, and dragging him to his feet as Mother Shipton pointed a finger at them.

The other three who'd come with them pushed past Miller and Marten without a second thought, leaving the pair who had dared speak with her to be surrounded by the hissing insects. The men screamed and batted at the mass in a futile manner, the moths seemingly unperturbed by flaming torches, weapons, or hands, intent on driving the men away.

Miller pushed Marten on, hissing as the moths' tiny, hooked feet tore into his hand. Blood poured from the wounds, and he gasped as the moth's sharp proboscis poked into it and drank deeply from the gashes. He stumbled and plunged the hand into the pool, crying out in shock at the cold water that enveloped his fingers for a second before Marten dragged him to his feet, and away from the cave with its dreaded pool.

The moths didn't pursue the men beyond the boundary of the path, leaving them to make their escape through the Forest, chased by the shadows of their imagination and the image of Mother Shipton's mirthless smile.

***

"Mother Shipton, Mother!" Anne called.

The woman in question smiled wryly at her maid's excited tone. The young woman had been something of a godsend since she'd permanently moved to the caves and called them home. As spry as she could be when she needed to be, the effects were only ever temporary, and her deformities limited her movement after a time regardless of her potions.

Anne had helped bring over the few items Mother Shipton had wanted from her old house; mostly sentimental items Toby had made, like their table, to furnish her new home. The girl kept the cave clean and went into town to save Mother Shipton from struggling her way there unless she had to. Plenty of people came to her, and those who *really* needed her would send a cart to fetch her from the Forest. They had a healthy respect for her, ever since Miller and his companions had dared to traipse through the Forest to threaten her. That, and the man had lost the use of his hand ever since he'd dipped it into the pool. The joints had frozen the next day, and he could no longer move his fingers. A curse, even if *she* hadn't performed it herself, retribution for the man thinking he was strong enough to take *her* on.

There was only *one* reason Anne would be this

excited. A dignitary must have been coming to see her for a prophecy like so many others had since her reputation had gone from strength to strength. Word had got around, spreading from the local gossips to those who travelled to York that heard what happened to the *previous* Lord Mayor. Whenever the prophecies took her, Mother Shipton recorded them for posterity, and the townsfolk whispered amongst themselves trying to decipher them. Of course, when her prophecies involved the *King* and the *Cardinal*, and of course came true, she became *the* soothsayer to seek out.

"Calm yourself, child, I'm here." She chuckled, reaching for her staff.

Her fingers caressed the smooth wood and she felt Toby's presence within the grain as she took hold of it and heaved herself onto her feet. Anne threw open the door that Miller had helped erect with a wall, alongside some of the other men from town, closing off the cave to the elements to create a proper home within the rock for her. The girl panted, clinging to the door handle, her other hand pressed to her stomach as she tried to catch her breath.

"Did you run all the way from town?" Mother Shipton chuckled; her staff clunked on the stone with each limped step towards her maid. "Who could *possibly* be coming to see me that has you in such a tizzy?"

Anne looked up sharply, her eyes wide, mouth open as she stared incredulously at the woman. "How did you know?"

"Because you only act this way when I have important guests. So, to whom do I owe the honour of a visit?"

"Cardinal *Wolsey* has come to seek you out," Anne whispered, glancing over her shoulder as if the mere utterance of his name might summon him forth.

"Himself?" Mother Shipton asked, raising her eyebrows.

"Not quite. He's sent an envoy, but rumour has it he may attend himself, depending on what you say to them."

Mother Shipton snorted with amusement, of course, the Cardinal hadn't come himself, he was too afraid of what might happen if he came in person. No doubt her conversation with the Abbot had reached the Cardinal's ears, and he hadn't liked what she said. The Cardinal expected to reside at York, as was his right, but her prophecies told her he'd never sit upon the seat he longed for, and he didn't like it. Though, like the Lord Mayor whose demise she'd predicted, she was merely the mouthpiece of fate where their stories were concerned.

"Who did he send?"

"I don't know them myself, but Mr Beasley is bringing them from York. He sent word ahead."

Mr Beasley. A mysterious man, but she knew who he was. How amusing that he would stick his nose into her business now and again, changing his name as it suited him. What games was the horned one playing now?

"Put another log on the fire, and make sure we have plenty of ale. We shall welcome our guests with open arms."

The cave bustled with activity as Anne and Mother Shipton readied themselves for their visitors. The moths that called the dark depths of the cavern home were abuzz with excitement of their own, infected by the ladies it seemed.

Night fell and the frantic movement stilled, the hush that came with their sudden halt made the rest of the world deafening. Mother Shipton sat in the rocking chair her husband had made for her, the soft carved wood embellished with moths of its own etched into the wood behind her head. Back and forth it rocked on curved legs, beside the fire, her shadow shrinking and growing with each tilt. She could feel Anne's excited nervousness, the poor girl had been a bundle of tremors all day since she'd brought news of the coming of the Cardinal's envoy. While Mother Shipton waited with calm amusement at the prospect.

Three sharp raps at the door caused Anne to almost jump out of her skin, and Mother Shipton smiled at the young maid as the girl glanced at her, waiting for the nod of permission. Rocking forward in her chair she used the momentum to propel her onto her feet, using her staff to steady herself as Anne hurried to open the door.

"Greetings, Miss, I am Mr. Beasley. My companions have come in search of counsel with Mother Shipton if she is willing to receive visitors at such an hour?" A deep male voice spoke from behind the partially opened door.

"Let them in, Anne, don't leave our guests outside in the cold. They've travelled a long way to be here. Come in, gentlemen, and make yourselves warm by the fire. Anne? Get them refreshments, girl, don't keep them waiting." Mother Shipton cooed to her maid as the girl opened the door and curtsied to the men as they stepped into the cave.

They looked awkward, glancing at one another and then at their guide, each one avoiding the gaze of the hunchbacked woman they'd come to see. Mr Beasley offered no names for his travelling companions, but she knew them all the same and knew all too well why they'd come to see her.

"Please, gentlemen, don't stand upon ceremony. Sit and warm yourselves, Anne will bring you all a drink." She reiterated, nodding to them as she sat back down.

"Mother Shipton, you would hardly make us welcome if you knew why we'd come." One spoke as he sat down, taking the empty tankard Anne offered as she scurried back into the firelight and handed one to each of the men.

Mother Shipton leaned forward in her chair and poured the man some ale from the jug Anne placed beside her, smiling as she did so. "My dear Duke of Suffolk, there's no reason why the messenger should be hanged." She said in a lilting tone.

The man jolted, surprised as she used his title even though no one had mentioned who they were, nor was any of them wearing anything that should have identified them. Mr Beasley stood behind the three dignitaries he'd brought to see her, sharing an amused smile as she caught his eye. Yes, she knew exactly who he had brought to see her, Mother Shipton knew far more than they would have liked. Charles Brandon, the Duke of Suffolk, Lord D'Arcy from Yorkshire, and Lord Percy the Earl of Northumberland.

"Look," Lord Percy snapped, all bravado with no substance, given his nervous shuffling and the suspicious eye he gave the mug of ale. "You know why we're here. You said to the Abbot that the Cardinal would never see York. He doesn't like it."

"I didn't say he would never see York." She replied amiably, turning her staff in her hands. "I said he *might* see York, but he would never reach it."

"Semantics." The Earl hissed, flinching as Mother Shipton cast a glance his way.

"Well," the duke turned his tankard in his hands uneasily. "He's saying that when he *does* come to York, you'll be burned at the stake."

Mother Shipton chuckled and unknotted the Married woman's kerchief from around her head, tossing it into the fire beside her.

The flames sprang to life, eagerly reaching out their red and orange tendrils to caress the material, but it remained untouched by the fire. She threw her staff onto the fire, where it too stayed free from harm. Without a second thought, she leaned forward and removed them from the hearth, as if reaching into a cool pool of water.

"If this had burned, I might have too." She shrugged, looking at the duke who stared at her in horror. "The time will come when you will be as low as I am, and that's low indeed."

Lord D'Arcy and Lord Percy glanced at one another and back at her before the Earl stammered at her. "D-do you know of *our* future?" He whispered.

"You'll be dead upon York's pavements." She smiled. "Good evening, gentlemen. Give my best to the Cardinal."

The moths overhead began to shift, the soft hush of their wings became a thunderous cacophony, and the three men couldn't get out of their seats fast enough. They dropped their tankards and scrambled over one another in their haste to escape, leaving Mr Beasley to tip his hat to Mother Shipton before he left more casually.

"Mother?" Anne muttered softly, a tone of panic in her voice.

"Go home, Anne, and do not return until I call for you." Mother Shipton said in a stern tone, turning to the young woman. "It would be safer that way."

Anne did not need to be told twice, and Mother Shipton was glad she didn't have to say more. Her maid hurried out of her home, leaving the prophetess alone with the shadows and her moths, preparing for the trouble coming her way.

She didn't have to wait long for the retribution she'd known would come from her latest prophecies. The Cardinal had threatened to burn her as a witch more than once, he hated everything she stood for, but since he'd fallen into her prophecies himself, she'd had a target placed upon her. He would've sent soldiers with his envoy, but he wouldn't threaten her without due cause. Now she'd given it to him. She'd reiterated her prophecy, and now she'd informed his cohorts of their own grizzly fate.

Standing outside the door to her home, shrouded in darkness, her eyes closed as she listened intently. The Forest was silent it seemed the whole *world* had fallen into silence as she waited for the men to arrive to kill her. Soft, careful footsteps crunched through the fallen leaves and twigs above. She counted at least six men, and she snorted.

"Only six, Cardinal? I'm insulted that you think so little of me."

No matter how careful they were, they could not hide the sound of their armour clinking against their weapons. They carried no torches, not wishing to alert her. How little they knew of her. She wondered if Mr Beasley was watching from somewhere to see what his daughter could do.

She held her staff before her and pulled herself as straight as she could. The shawl around her shoulders hummed and shifted, the moths crawled and crowded across her torso in an ever-moving mass. The first of the soldiers shuffled quietly around the edge of the pool, eyes drawn to the smooth water, following the soothing drips to the petrified plants that hung over the outcropping. They'd clearly heard rumours of the Petrifying Well, but being this close to it unnerved the men.

"Good evening, gentlemen. I see you've come to follow through on the Cardinal's promise to end my life." She whispered, her voice ethereal, stirring the moths that all but cocooned her upper body.

"That's right, *witch*, you shall make no more threats." Your allegiance with the Devil ends here." The lead soldier snarled, hand upon his musket as he aimed the weapon at her chest.

"Oh, my dear boy, how naive. Your Cardinal has sent you to meet your end, and he shall meet his own soon enough. My prophecy will remain true, even if I die, so he will gain nothing by my death. Though, unfortunately for you, I have not the patience to dally with you tonight. Shall we end this swiftly? For your sake, rather than my own, it's not your fault you follow that fool."

The men sneered at her and stood in formation; muskets raised as she smiled. With what strength she had she lifted her staff and brought it down with a resounding bang. The sound echoed off the rocks as if all six muskets had been shot all at once. A ripple ran over the mirror-like surface of the pool and the ground shook beneath the soldiers' feet. The moths covering her body flittered away, in a hissing tornado of bodies. They whirled around her head for a moment, waiting for permission. With a nod of her head, they swarmed the soldiers.

Their screams were muffled by the mass of insects as the moths surrounded and strangled the men who had come to harm their mistress. The soldiers dropped their weapons to bat at the insects, clawing at their throats as they gasped for air, starved of oxygen as the tiny wing scales filled their mouths and clogged their lungs. One of the men stumbled out of the cloud and fell into the pool; the moment he resurfaced and reached for the edge to pull himself out, he stopped.

Mother Shipton stepped towards him, watching his eyes grow wide as he slowly extended a hand to her for help. She cocked her head to one side as the realisation began to settle on his face, his mouth opened in agonising slowness. He let out one last rasping gasp of air before the terrified expression froze on his face for all eternity.

A smile crossed her face as she looked back at the other soldiers, all pushed towards the pool by the moths, and the dripping water of the Well. The moment the water touched them the process began, sped up by her presence and the influence of her beloved moths.

It started slowly, solidifying the spot the water had touched, creeping through the rest of their bodies. The creaking sound of stone rubbing against stone grew louder as the soldiers fought against the inevitable, until their limbs no longer could move, and their lungs turned to stone Their last breaths froze in their throats, some clinging to them as if they could pull the stone out, the others screaming in silent fear.

Once the last soldier transitioned, the moths' deep thrum subsided and the cloud dissipated, leaving Mother Shipton amongst her living stature. A horned shadow lingered out of the corner of her eye as she reached out and tapped the head of each soldier, shattering the stone into rubble and gravel that scattered across the pathway of her home.

It would serve as an alarm should anyone think to try and sneak up on her. Then again, who would dare cross Mother?

THE END

THE LEGEND OF TOM MCCOY
By Dawn DeBraal

The night sky was lit up by a great fire that danced in the middle of the gathering spot. Hard-working villagers were drawn like moths around the flames holding their hands out and rubbing them to keep warm on the crisp fall evening by harvesters, gleaning what was left behind in the fields. The landowner let them come for free, for it was a sin to waste food. At day's end, every person gathered around the fire to celebrate the harvest with merriment and stories.

Benjamin Berlay, owner of the fields, smiled upon the group who gathered on his farm. They would stay the night, and share in the festivities as part of the harvest ritual. Tents were set up, an annual tradition, while children played tag in the dark. Where did they get their energy?

A large cauldron of soup simmered above the fire made from roasted rutabagas, squash, onions, and a few chickens that Benjamin contributed. The smell permeated the air as the warm soup was ladled into cups and bowls of those present.

An orange moon known as the harvest moon hung in the sky reminding the people that the winter months were coming, and they should prepare themselves for the long, dark, and cold season.

"Mr. Berlay, tell us a story," the children begged. Every year the same thing. The farmer would set the people down to recite the legend of Tom McCoy in his thick Irish accent. Everyone loved the story and hung on to his every word. Benjamin laughed and drew them near. People sat on sacks, stumps, and baskets, anxious to hear the legend, forgotten from the year before.

Benjamin lit his pipe and pulled in the sweet tobacco exhaling, sat upon a large stump speaking in a voice that was loud and clear, commanding the attention of every listener.

"Poor Tom McCoy, he lived down the road a ways," Benjamin swept his hand toward the old, abandoned farm next door. "Tom was a dedicated farmer though he didn't know enough about this area after buying that haunted place from a fleeing family. The Turners left in the middle of the night, claiming the ghost of a witch by the name of Camela Pert wouldn't leave the farm." The children gasped, especially the younger ones.

"A witch!" they whispered, their eyes large, adding to the excitement Benjamin was building.

"Tom had his own way of doing things even after he was told to plant cold crops because the growing season here in the north is short. But old Tom, he just wouldn't listen. He gambled year after year losing his crops to the frost. The bank was ready to take his farm for defaulting on the loan. Tom was put to the test and had failed miserably. We all felt sorry for the man, trying to help him as best we could, but he was stubborn and wouldn't listen. It was his way or no way at all." Berlay let that part sink in. Children should learn to do as they are told or face the consequences.

"The farm fell into disrepair for the man had no money to fix the broken things. Tom needed help, and in desperation he conjured the witch that lived on the farm, raising Camela Pert from the dead.

Camela's house was unique for a house in the woods. It was not a simple cabin, but a monstrosity, with spires, gargoyles, and cupulas. The kinds of things that haunted castles are made of. After the "spell" she put on the McCoy Farm, the house grew darker. The sun couldn't penetrate the trees, mildew and mould covered the siding. People who visited said the house was never warm inside and uninviting on the outside. One day, Tom's wife and children disappeared off the face of the earth. The house reflected the poison that Tom McCoy had created when he exchanged his family for fortune. Camela Pert demanded payment for casting a spell on the fields to grow his crops to fruition and Old Tom McCoy was said to agree to her terms. You see he was desperate to save the farm and would do almost anything Camela asked him. He had been bewitched."

Everyone looked at one another with open mouths and the shadows of the fire danced upon their faces casting a ghostly image on each face. Berlay smiled. His story was taking effect he could feel his audience softening, preparing them.

"Knowing he had witchcraft on his side, Tom planted all the wrong crops for this area again. Amazingly, the rains came at the right time, the frost held off in an unusually mild fall and he was able to make a living on that farm for the first time. Cucumbers, tomatoes, and watermelons flourished in his fields when the frost should have bitten them well before they could be harvested. It was nothing short of magic. Dark magic to be sure. Tom had sold his soul."

The children gasped again, this made Benjamin smile. He took pleasure in recanting the story of a farmer who had gone down the wrong path and would pay for his sins.

"The house grew darker, reflecting the condition of Tom McCoy's soul, until no one felt they could approach the dark place for fear of taking the evil home and welcoming it into their homes. Passersby claimed to see a woman and young boys, believed to be Matilda McCoy and her sons, but upon approaching the foul ground, the apparitions disappeared. Evil had taken hold of Tom. For seven years, McCoy had the best harvest in Youngsville, growing crops that would never make it otherwise. We thought because of his success, his wife and children would return in the flesh for he told people Matilda left with the children when his farm was going under. But they did not come back despite his claim they would return. The town still waited for their joyful reunion, but when no word came from Tom's family, suspicions grew. Something was oddly wrong at the McCoy farm. Trees surrounding the house were dying of disease, and the last year he was alive, everything froze, and Tom went bankrupt. The favour of Camela Pert had run its time.

Curious folk began trespassing on Tom's property looking for the graves of Matilda and her two sons, Joe, and Mac. Because they believed Tom had bargained with the witch."

Again, the children gasped. Berlay had them in the palm of his hand. He tapped his pipe on the stump emptying the ash and put it in his bib pocket, then took a swig from the jug sitting next to the stump and cleared his throat.

"In the middle of the night, Tom used to wait for the bank officers convinced they were coming to chase him off his property. He would shoot his gun in the air to scare off the intruders, but when the bank saw the condition of the house, there wasn't much to take, for the house was caving in, alive with the animals of the forest. It wasn't the bankers Tom was shooting at, but troublemaking kids, young'uns about your age, trying to scare the strange man." He pointed at the children.

"Even though Tom pointed his shotgun in the air, some of the fragments exploded and a young girl, Sarah Anne Hucksway caught some metal in the eye. She screamed and the children ran off leaving her to stumble in the dark woods trying to find her way home.

The dead trees moaned and creaked in the wind, and the sound of owls and night animals scared the little girl who got hopelessly lost after the children ran away leaving her to fend on her own. When the young ones got back to town, her parents discovered Sarah Anne was missing, and her father went out to search for his little girl.

Hucksway called his daughter's name as he walked

through the woods. The moon barely peeked through the dense dead trees, and he feared the worst when he heard her small cry. Hucksway turned to face the sound and found his daughter in the arms of a woman he suspected was Matilda McCoy, though he had not seen the woman in years, she hadn't changed but for her eyes that were black holes in her head, and she was covered in vines.

"Let her go!" Hucksway commanded. The ghost of Matilda put Sarah down and disappeared into the fog. The angry father claimed that he saw Matilda and the boys standing in the woods being held back by vines that seemed to hold them in place. McCoy levelled his shotgun at the man demanding he leave the property, the father didn't argue with McCoy, grabbing his little girl, he ran. Tom McCoy's craziness had become a menace to everyone."

"How come the town didn't run off McCoy?" shouted one of the teenagers. Berlay looked up at the boy and packed his pipe again. Taking a small stick and holding it to the fire lighting his tobacco, squinted at the teen giving him such a look that the boy settled back on the seed bag and quieted down.

"Tom had become paranoid after that and took to staying awake at night, sitting on his front porch with a shotgun laid across his lap watching for trespassers. On more than one occasion he was seen talking to people that weren't there. Those stories got back to the village where the man had become unstable. During the day McCoy still tried to work hard on that farm that wouldn't turn a profit, but at night he barely slept in a chair jumping at every little sound. And there were plenty of those, between the crows, raccoons, and rats, he was waking up and shooting in the air several times a night. You could hear the racket, and we all figured the man had gone mad from the lack of sleep. The lucky spell from Camela Pert had run its course, and the final payment was due. More than McCoy's wife and children, Tom had to give up his soul too.

People in the village saw the change in McCoy. His skin became papery, thin, and dry. His lips burned by the sun peeled. Tom was listless and weak talking out of his head, making no sense. One of his neighbours, Ham Crocker, took it upon himself to go out to talk to Tom, trying to appeal to the man to give up his secret and tell them where Matilda and the boys were. He told the farmer that confessing the sin of murder would help Tom's soul to heal. Ham offered to uncover their graves and bury the McCoy's proper near a church, in hallowed ground."

"Did he show them where his family was?" asked a little boy. Berlay shook his head no.

"Alas, Ham didn't return, nor was he ever seen or heard from again!" The anxious crowd's mouths dropped open at the thought of the McCoy farm now being haunted by several people.

"Gossip was on the tongues of everyone. As it grew, people had to know what happened to Matilda and her sons and of course, Tom's neighbour, Ham. They gathered in town with torches and raised such a ruckus they went out in the middle of the night to find Tom hanging on the pole like a scarecrow, with a murder of crows pecking at his dead body." Berlay stood extending his arms as if he were tied to a cross piece on a pole letting the visual sink in.

"They took poor McCoy's body down from the scarecrow pole and buried it deep in the woods. After that, they kept seeing Camela Pert, who was long dead. She was seen along with Ham, Tom McCoy, his boys, and Matilda, frolicking in a child's game under the light of the moon." The children screeched at this part, it made Berlay laugh, they had become putty in his hands. The old farmer could see the look of concern on the parents' faces. He knew they wanted him to back off on the scary parts of the story, their children would have nightmares. But Berlay wanted to do the story justice and there was a moral lesson to be learned here. The incident he told was real and happened just outside their village. It was mandatory that he do this tale, and in the right way so that Camela Pert could harvest a villager who was being put under her spell as he spoke. It was her fair share of his successful bounty on his property, and it was required.

The littlest children were whisked away to their tents and put to sleep by wary parents. They would not remember this story the next day and would be excited as if it were the first time they'd heard the legend of Tom McCoy, under the next harvest moon.

With magic, people forgot the story because of the spell Camela Pert put upon them. To hear the tale and remember it would send the people away, never to return. This was part of the gleaning process. The story told, people warned, only to forget and fall prey to Camala's charms. Berlay was spared this forgetfulness, for he was part of the legend.

"Now that McCoy was dead, we went out to his farm and beat back the bushes with sticks looking for the graves of Matilda and her sons. Beneath an old lilac bush, the skeletal hand of Matilda pointed to the shallow graves of her sons."

While everyone was focused on Berlay, the woods around them filled with fog that slowly wormed its way through the crowd, winding up the gleaners' legs like vines, whispering in their ears paralyzing them where they stood.

Camela exited the woods, followed by Matilda, Joe, and Mac, close behind them was Ham Crocker, along with the missing woman Sarah, from last year, only no one remembered her as missing, they remembered that a rearing horse killed her. The last to leave the safety of the woods was Tom McCoy. The ghosts wore clothing that was torn, their flesh falling from their bones, only Camela Pert looked whole.

People screamed and shouted but were unable to move because they'd been frozen in place by the vines that held them fast. The ghostly crew circled about the crowd to pick the person they wanted to take in this year's harvest. Berlay chuckled. He loved this part, and then without a warning they chose.

"Wait! No!" Berlay shouted, for it was none other than his oldest boy, Samuel, who slowly followed Camela Pert into the fog that drifted back into the woods. The rest of the ghostly crew circled the crowd whispering in their ears that it was time to go to sleep and that they did not see what they saw.

Parents rushed their children into tents, and other folks not feeling right, left to go home with their harvest, until all that remained was the farmer on the stump in front of a dying fire. Camela released him whispering in his ear.

"Good night, children," Berlay said tapping his pipe on the stump. He had been assured another good harvest next year because Camela Pert got what she wanted, forgetting it was his son who had been picked this year. Camela had changed Benjamin Berlay's memory, he had also been bewitched.

Time and tales were twisted and warped to Camela's bidding. She looked into her crystal ball searching for a new storyteller, for Berlay's time was up. Successful crops for seven years, the deal she had made, and Camela had held her end of the bargain, now it was Berlay's turn.

The farmer woke from the night feeling ill, and sad at the death of his son, Samuel, earlier that year having been caught in a piece of farm machinery. The farmer couldn't remember where his son was buried. Wasn't that strange?

He walked outdoors to use the hand pump in front of the house. The cold water rushed over his hands as he splashed it on his face, grabbing the towel hanging on the branch and wiping away the water when his eyes spied a horse and wagon coming up the road, he shook his head in disgust. His son Peter had come a day late and a dollar short, as always.

"Peter. Harvest Night was last night. I'm afraid you have nothing to glean." Peter looked at his dishevelled father and chuckled.

"You are wrong father. I was summoned."

"Summoned? By whom?"

"Camela Pert." Berlay felt a sharp pain in his chest and his hands went to his heart.

"No, I have another year yet, at least," he told his son.

"No father, this was the seventh year, she told me in a dream."

"Don't take her offer, whatever you do, son. You are young. Let another old man take up the gleaning of the souls."

"Don't worry Father I already turned it down. There will be seven more gleaners before it is my turn. I have another forty-nine years, at least. Berlay fell to one knee trying to pull himself up on the pump, but he was too weak.

"Camela, face me and do this. Don't be a coward, let my son go." Berlay shouted to the sky. The fog came from the woods slowly inching its way across the newly gleaned fields and swirled around Berlay who was still on one knee trying to catch his breath and stop his heart from pounding out of his chest. He looked up to see Camela, the McCoy family, along with Ham Crocker, and then he saw his wife and son gasping at the clarity of truth. His eldest son had been harvested last night.

But most surprising was his wife standing next to Samuel.

"Cora? You were harvested? Why don't I remember that? You took sick with the fever." Cora's head shook side to side slowly as she reached for her husband, her hand touched his face, and Berlay slumped to the ground while his son Peter, looked on.

Camela was tired having spent the night wiping out memories of what took place during story hour on the farm. The townspeople left this morning satisfied with their wagons full of food, none the wiser. They would be back next year, listening to the new storyteller she had selected. She told Peter the truth, that he had seven years when he accepted the job. He told her he wanted seven times seven, shaking Camela's hand. She told him no, but he forgot that part after she whispered in his ear.

THE END

THE PARROT MAN
By John Clewarth

Every kid gets scared of something, whether it comes out of a bad dream or perhaps one of those stories kids tell each other in the schoolyard, to spook one another. My childhood fear came from both these things and more. Looking down the curve of houses where I grew up, I can see nothing much has changed. Apart from the satellite dishes on just about every wall, a few more cars and everything looking smaller to my grown-up eyes, the place looks as if it's been frozen in time. For most people that might feel all cosy and safe – a reminder of simpler, more protected times. Not for me.

I was born and brought up just there, number 152 Etcham Crescent. My Dad was a coal miner, my mum died giving birth to me. So, Dad brought me up on his own. Of course, there was my big brother, Eddie, too. Everyone worshipped Eddie. He was to follow Dad straight into the pit, like most lads did at that time – you know, before the pits were all shut down by the government. Yeah, everybody worshipped Eddie – except me. Don't get me wrong, it wasn't that I didn't look up to him. I wanted to be the way he was; charm the birds out of the trees and all that. But he saved all his charm for everyone except me.

I mean, your big brother should keep you under his wing. At least that's the way it was for all my friends. But he crushed me every chance he had. Got away with it, too, like he did everything else. He always messed around at school but the teachers just described him as a 'likeable rogue'. 'A chip off the old block, eh Mr White?' They didn't know what he was really like. Took everyone in, did Eddie.

When I say everyone worshipped Eddie, there was this one kid; tubby lad with pock-scarred skin. He was three years older than me, but shorter than most of the kids in my year group. Mark Skidwell, his name was. Eddie called him Skidmark and it stuck. It was the reaction he got from the kid that made him do it even more; Mark Skidwell just blubbed, then went and grassed to the teachers. They did nothing about it, of course – bullying was rife in those days, and 'mental health and well-being' hadn't even been invented yet. From then on, it was a push here, a trip there, pages mysteriously ripped from Skidmark's textbooks, post-it notes with 'Kick me, I'm a saddo' written on, stuck on the poor kid's back.

The cronies were more than happy to follow Eddie

and join in with his larks. The only one who didn't laugh was Skidmark. And me. Well, I pretended to. I dared not do anything else. But I knew how it felt to be the focus of Eddie's attention, the butt of his jokes. Mind you, you need to understand that although Eddie wasted his time at school, he wasn't thick. No... He was cunning, like a fox. Aside from the physical stuff, he could just as effectively get inside your head.

He resented me since the day I was born. It'd be easy to think it was because Mum died during childbirth. But I know he was just born bad. Saw me as the cuckoo in his nest and wasn't happy to share. I was a trespasser on his patch, stealing attention from him. And Eddie thrived on attention. Dad just thought I was accident-prone: 'You're so clumsy, always toppling over like old Jackie Sedgeway!' Jackie was the local spook; every town had one in those days, right? The one the parents told their kids to keep away from, because 'he just wasn't right'. Jackie lived on his own, never worked and drank a lot, hence he fell over a lot, too. His face was scarred from getting caught in a fire when he was a child. So, he looked different. And being different, in our town, made you vulnerable.

When I tried to talk to Dad about my problems, he said I should stop being jealous of my big brother, and make some mates, like Eddie did. I tried, but I was no good at making friends. I was naturally quiet and I became increasingly withdrawn, as Eddie wiped his feet on my self-esteem, immune to any repercussions from Dad or teachers. I didn't resent the adults for this; after all, Eddie was so believable, *so plausible,* so damn *likeable!* Always got what he wanted from Dad, too. That damn motorbike with its stinking 2-stroke petrol, Dad got him that – even though he was too young. Dad said it was too good a deal to turn down, and his mate had wanted a quick sale. He told Eddie he should wait till his birthday before riding it. That was never gonna happen. He was riling the hell out of the neighbours, bozzing around on it at all hours, right from the get-go. Just gave his cheeky smile, when they caught up with him, and said it wouldn't happen again. Yeah, Eddie had a real talent for making people believe he was a rough diamond; a mischievous but good guy. He was adept at planting seeds in people's heads, you see. Except, he planted different seeds in my mind.

When most big brothers were looking out for their little siblings, mine was warping my brain. One morning before school – I was about seven - while I was eating my cornflakes, he told me about the rabid dog that waited at the top of the stairs, just around the corner on the landing – the bit you couldn't see, just outside my bedroom door. He said not to tell Dad, cos grown-ups wouldn't be able to see it. I fretted through the day at school, seeing snarling shadows and shapes in each doorway and in every dark cupboard. At bedtime, I made my milk and biscuits last as long as possible, till Dad gave me enough grief to shift me. Eddie had gone up early, 'to do his homework'. Yeah, right.

Climbing the stairs on tiptoe and holding my breath, my ears were keened for every sound. Old, framed photos in gloomy black and white hung on the stairwell wall; bought by Mum before I finished her off, these showed images of Stonefeather village in the olden days. They did nothing to dispel my unease. Foolishly, I forgot all about the top step – the creaky one. It was loud enough to wake the dead as I trod on it tonight. I froze, blood rushing in my ears. Hardly daring to look up, but knowing I must, I checked the landing for signs of movement. Nothing. I strained my ears for tell-tale noises; just the drip, drip, drip of the bathroom tap that Dad had been 'getting fixed' for over a year now.

The last pussy-foot-step up to the landing was like setting foot on thin ice, on the verge of a precipice. All clear! I sighed – *such glorious relief.* No rabid dogs here! I pushed open my bedroom door. A crouching shape in the darkness. Ready to spring. A guttural growl – and the thing was upon me. I fell back onto the landing, pinned down by the grinning, *barking* form of Eddie. He must have been there for an hour or more. He was dedicated to his torment of me. To this day, I open my bedroom door slowly, checking for concealed monsters in the dark.

'Only one way to get rid of it for absolute certain,' Eddie offered a half-hope, one afternoon, as we bumped along home on the school bus. 'You have to stop the bathroom tap dripping. That's what attracts the rabid dog.'

'That was you just messing about. There was no dog!'

He shrugged. 'Wasn't there *that* night – that's true. But he *was* sniffin' around outside. Always hangs about when the tap's drip-drip-dripping.' Then he turned his head away and just looked out of the window, at the passing shops and pubs. Another seed sown. I knew that, tonight, I had to do what Dad hadn't done in a year.

I had to stop the tap.

So, there I was, gargling and rinsing after brushing my teeth. And there he was. 'Stop dawdling then. Go on,' Eddie said, a tinge of mockery in his voice. 'Give the tap a good squeeze – *real* good. I reckon that'll stop it dripping.'

I placed my hand on the fawcett, ready to twist clockwise with all my might. I took a deep breath and as I was about to do it, Eddie said, 'Only problem is, if you squeeze the handle any tighter, the spider that lives in the tap will come running out.'

I pulled my hand away quicker than a blink, turning to look at him with wide, frightened eyes. *Spiders!* I was – still am – seriously phobic about them; their horrible unfeasibly long legs, fat, squelchy, hairy little bodies and weird, multiple eyes. But, most of all, it was the way they ran. Fast and furious!

'Oh, yeah,' he whispered. 'And once it sees you, it'll chase you into your room and get in bed with you. Crawl into your ear, in the night, and lay its eggs, right there. You'll hear the little pillocks hatching out and burrowing into your brain.'

I shot into my room, slamming the door behind me. I could hear Eddie guffawing loudly in the bathroom.

Again, to this very day, I never overtighten taps for fear of what may come scuttling out. I began to sleep less and less well, and when I did, bad dreams plagued my slumber; nightmares of hunched forms in the dark, or savage, multi-eyed dogs with frothing jaws and too many legs skittering towards me, smothering my face as I lay helpless in bed.

He was a sadist, Eddie was, with a cruel talent for implanting terrible notions in my impressionable mind. So, it will come as no surprise, that when he first mentioned the Parrot Man to me, the idea took up residence front and centre in my thoughts. But there was one difference this time: he actually had some 'evidence' for his nasty story.

He made me sit and watch a badly put-together PowerPoint presentation that he'd done for English at school. The students had been told they could present on any subject they wanted, and for once, he did his homework – seeing an irresistible chance to make some trouble. He chose an old urban myth about the Parrot Man of Stonefeather and its outlying districts. He'd found links to obscure little websites that obsessed about it. He told me the Parrot Man stalked the streets after dark, picking off local kids one by one.

Why was he given that name? Eddie said the Parrot Man was well-known, a crazy old guy who would grab unruly youngsters, or innocent ones if all else failed. He would peck their eyes from their heads with his beak-like mouth, and strangle them with wiry hands that were covered in scales or fur, depending on which website you visit. I wanted to tell him to kiss my ass and that he was spouting crap again, but like I said, the seed was already planted in my psyche.

Sightings had come from the early 1930s and then raised their heads again in the 1960s – as if the Parrot Man hibernated or something.

The story goes that just one kid was lucky enough to escape, and he gave a rough description of what the guy looked like. Eddie showed me a slide of a faded colour drawing he'd found on the net. It was nightmarish; an artist's impression of a man-shaped thing, uncommonly tall, with strangely long arms ending in claw-like hands. It wore a feather-covered cloak, resembling unholy wings. Cruel and beady black eyes looked out from a face that had no nose, save for a flat flap of withered skin; instead, it was the jawline that jutted out, like the beak of an octopus – or a parrot. It stood, hunched in a crouch, as if always ready to pounce...

When I say the kid was lucky to escape, that's purely relative. Eddie said the Parrot Man had gotten away with his right eye – and the kid had never been able to escape the nightmares, having emotional problems for the rest of his life. Eddie also gleefully explained that the Parrot Man would leave brightly-coloured feathers in the seeping sockets of his victims' eyes.

When I told Dad that Eddie had been scaring me with this, he told me to lighten up. He said those kinds of websites are run by geeky little losers with nothing but imaginary friends – all made up to scare stupid little kids like me. Eddie could do no wrong in his eyes and, worst of all, the English teacher actually gave him a commendation for his sick project; and praised him for his *enthusiasm and commitment*. That's right, Eddie was getting rewarded for tormenting me.

Eddie had leaned in real close, so I could smell his stinking breath. 'If you look at the dates when Parrot Man's been popping up and *popping out eyes*,' he snickered at his own joke, 'then I reckon he's due to come back any time now.'

Back at school, he really milked this with Skidmark; the coloured feathers left in his locker were the least of them. Skidmark's 'locker' didn't actually lock: the padlock had been jemmied off so many times, he had given up replacing it. But at least it closed. The fake eyeball (a ping pong ball, painted and daubed with strawberry jam) was fairly original, accompanied by a typed note, reading, 'You're next – love Parrot Man'. But the most repulsive prank was the raw liver left in there, signalling its presence by thick, oozy blood seeping from the gap at the bottom. Skidmark actually ran off that day. Police had to be called to look for him – they found him later, just hanging around the bus station, looking blank and dishevelled.

'He 'specially likes pecking at fat kids like you,' Eddie smirked, passing him in the canteen, the week before half term. 'I think old Parrot Man will've worked up a big old appetite by now. Almost Halloween, Skidders. I can see you've been getting ready early, yeah? Why don't you take the mask off?'

Skidmark's eyes welled up with tears, as he pushed a piece of tomato round his plate with his fork. Poor sod was always trying to lose weight and ate nothing but salads at school. 'What's up, chubs, can't you manage the tomato? Somebody put you off your fodder?' One of Eddie's hangers-on grinned widely at his own sarcasm.

'Nah,' Eddie came back quick. 'He's just leaving enough room for his pigswill later.'

A tear rolled down Skidmark's cheek and Eddie ruffled his hair. 'Don't worry, my old pork sausage – Parrot Man'll come get you on Halloween – peck out your piggy little eyeballs.' He swaggered off with his band of yes-boys, in a thick cloud of cruel laughter.

My year group was just coming into lunch. I was tempted to sit with him – he was always on his own. I wanted to tell him that Eddie picked on me, too. That he made me feel like something he had stepped in on the sidewalk. That I wished I could have any big brother but him. But instead, I sat at another table, which was almost full, and was soon surrounded by the comforting company of neutral strangers.

* * *

I'd seen Eddie in a huddle with his sidekicks, just about every breaktime at school for days now. They'd disappear outside straight after they'd fed their faces, and hunker around one of the picnic benches, furthest away from the school building. Either that, or they were sloping off to the Art Room, shutting the door behind them. Eddie was up to something and it was guaranteed to be nasty. It looked like he was roping his buddies in to help him this time. I'd have to be on my guard. It was half term the following week, and Halloween fell on the Wednesday. I figured his masterstroke would happen then and it would feature that bloody Parrot Man somehow. I was right; well, almost right.

He'd been really nice to me during the first few days of the holiday. Suspiciously nice. If I hadn't known what a total ass he was, I would have thought he'd had a miracle personality transplant. I'd made up my mind that, for the first time ever, I wasn't going Trick or Treating on Halloween. Then he wouldn't be able to pull any of his stunts on me.

Tuesday was fish and chip night and, as ever, it was me who had to go out and get them. It was cold as the grave, with the kind of rain that seeps through your clothes like icy pellets whipping in the wind. It sounded all the louder as it pelted my hood. The street lights were all off, the latest money-saving venture of our parish council; Dad said the money they saved would just go to more free lunches for the councillors to feed their big, fat faces with. The chippie was several streets away from us – and the route there passed by the house of the local misfit, Jackie Sedgeway. His house had been egged, had dog mess shoved through the letter box, and had cruel messages daubed on his door so many times that if the poor guy wasn't round the bend to start with, he would almost certainly have been driven there.

I looked across from the other side of the street; always the other side of the street when you walked past old Jackie's. His place was in darkness, but I saw the net curtains twitch and a squat shadow creeping away into safer darkness. *Christ,* what an existence for the guy.

It was as I turned the corner onto Hollerton Drive that I saw the Parrot Man.

There, at the far end of the street, skulking in the shadows of the smashed-up bus shelter. I froze. He wasn't moving, wasn't even looking in my direction – but it was unmistakably him; the long, talon-like fingers, the weird protuberance from the face, and the cloak billowing in the wind. I was about to turn around, go back the way I'd come, get back home and dry.

But how would I explain to Dad? Returning home empty-handed, with tales of a mythical monster lurking in the streets? Then another thought hit me: Eddie had been out all day. He must have been loitering about for who knew how long, just waiting for his stupid chance to get me; a little curtain-raiser ahead of his main Halloween performance. *That's what he'd been cooking up with his crazy mates!* Well, this time, his prank would fall flat on its sorry backside. Pulling my hood tight, I continued walking; *I wasn't Mark Skidmore*, and I wasn't putting up with his scare tactics any longer.

I'd gone a few steps, when the half-hunched figure turned, looking in my direction. And my courage evaporated. What if it wasn't Eddie? What if it really was the..? My heart began to double-time, throbbing in my own ears beneath the hood.

Noooo! The figure started moving in my direction. Perhaps he hadn't seen me? I ducked into the nearest garden and crouched down behind the hedge, almost gashing myself on a broken bottle. Peering through the scanty branches, I could see Parrot Man getting closer, casting no shadow, just an extension of the darkness.

I stuffed my fist in my mouth, to stop myself from whimpering. What if it wasn't Eddie..? I had a strong urge to scream out loud and run. The creature was just a couple of gates away; it peered upwards, seeming to sniff the air. *Jesus, it's gonna smell me out!* It raised a barbed hand. *This is it: The Parrot Man's found me!* I screwed my eyes shut, as if this would be some defence against the beast that would suck them out from my head. Footsteps – right on the other side of the hedge. I felt sick and I trembled like a new-born kitten. I swear, at that moment, I almost heard my sanity snap.

'Let's go join the others.' The glee in Eddie's voice was intense. My mind whirled and my eyes snapped open, as he added, 'That dork's never gonna sleep again, after tonight!'

'Let's do it! Is Tommo round the back already?' Another voice, hushed and excited. I looked out from under my hood, to see that the figure had been joined by another.

'Yeah, all going to plan! Come on, let's go spook us a pig!'

I forced myself to watch as the two figures crossed the street. Momentarily, I could make no sense of this. It now seemed there were *two* Parrot Men, and yet, I had heard Eddie's voice. I watched them stop at a gate, further up and saw another couple of heads pop out from the side of the house. That's when it registered. Eddie and his mates from school! They'd all got themselves dressed in costumes; that's what all the visits to the Art Room had been about – a freaky flock of Parrot Men.

I could see now that the outfits were made up from old bits and scraps – when you looked clearly, you could see the crappy joins. But from a distance, and in the first few seconds up close, the illusion was so real.

My emotions were a concoction of relief – I'd been scared to death I was gonna die, a minute ago; anger, and pure pity. Pity for the *pig* that would be getting spooked. The house they were targeting was Mark Skidmore's. Skidmark was in for it tonight. I didn't even go back onto the street. Clambering over fences and hedges, I stuck to the relative safety of gardens, until the shadows swallowed me up – and I ran.

* * *

Bedraggled and smelling of sweat, I sneaked in through the back door. Dad had the TV on loud and was cursing the referee at the football game. I managed to get upstairs unnoticed. Even if I hadn't missed out on the creaking top step, I'm sure Dad wouldn't have heard me; aside from the racket on the TV, he'd be on his third or fourth beer by now. I shut my bedroom door and barricaded it with my bedside table. Drying myself off as well as I could with an old tee shirt, I pulled on some fresh clothes, bundling my dirty clothes under the bed.

I heard another stream of raucous abuse from downstairs, as the referee got yet another decision wrong. If Dad discovered I'd come back without his supper, he'd have my hide for a hearth rug. I sat with my back against my bed, knees drawn up to my chest. Taking deep, shuddering breaths, I tried to calm myself enough to go down and talk to him. He had to understand I was too damn scared to go out there – Eddie and his mates were out for trouble and I didn't want to get caught up in the middle of it. Dad would just have to understand – and actually *do something* about Eddie.

I heard the screaming before I heard the banging on the front door. Stumbling to my feet, I went to the window and saw Eddie on the path. He was staggering round, one hand flapping wildly in the air, the other clutching at his eye. He ran again at the door and kicked at it, once, twice, three times!

'Go round the back, the door's open! And stop flaming banging on the door, or I'll knock some sense into your head. The fish and chips'll be cold!' Dad thought it was me, back from the supper errand.

I watched on, mesmerised, as Eddie continued to flap around, his stupid costume tattered and torn. Maybe Skidmark had given him more than he bargained for. He reeled towards the side of the yard and yanked the canvas off his motorbike, all the time looking around like something was hunting him; I laughed quietly – he looked as if he was winking with his right eye. Something was badly wrong. Should I go tell Dad? But the mood he was in, he'd have beaten the pair of us black and blue.

Eddie fired up the Kawasaki, shaking his head madly as if trying to dislodge something. Then he slithered out through the open gate, rubber squealing as the tyres slid and slipped. He somehow steadied the bike and, once on the road, rushed through the gears, speeding out of sight around the curve at the top of the street.

* * *

I sat in the darkest corner of my room, knees drawn up to my chest. Eddie had by now been gone ages, the football match on TV had finished, and Dad was ranting and raving downstairs. He sounded as if he was throwing furniture around. I panicked, threw my arms to my head in an attempt to block it all out, and in so doing knocked over the chair by my bed. It hit the floor with a resounding bump.

'What?!' Dad growled, like some kind of wild

animal. 'Get yourself down here, now!'

Ohmygod, ohmygod, he'd heard me! I didn't dare disobey him and stay where I was; the thought of him coming upstairs terrified me. I had to go down and face the music.

From the top of the landing, I could see his furious face glaring up at me and, trembling, I began to descend. I'd made it halfway down when there was a loud knocking at the door again. *Thank God, Eddie. For once in your life, you've done me a favour!*

Dad whirled around and flipped the lock off the door, yanking it open. A burly policeman stood there, accompanied by a female officer. Dad stood there, slack-jawed.

'Mr White, I'm afraid we have some bad news.' Dad slumped to his knees as if he'd been clubbed on the head, gaping up as the police delivered the news. Eddie had gone full throttle down the main road and smashed into a trailer that was coming out from a side road. The impact was fast and hard – his body went under the truck, and his head parted company, sailing over the flatbed and bouncing more than a hundred yards before coming to a stop against a tree. When they found it, he still had on that fake cardboard beak, secured with an elastic band. The police said something had torn out one of his eyes.

They arrested Jackie Sedgeway that same night. Apparently, he howled and whined like a dog as they bundled him into the police car and a jeering crowd began to gather. Eddie and his gang had been seen off by Skidmark's dad before they'd even had a chance to get started on him. Deciding not to waste the evening, they had opted to put the frighteners on old Jackie. Big brother had stood at the front door, the others round the sides, awaiting his signal. Eddie had shouted some unwholesome things through the letterbox and had begun to batter the door loudly. The moment Jackie came out, he would be confronted by the infamous 'Parrot Man' – then a progeny of others would emerge from all sides.

It was when they heard Eddie's screams of agony that they realised something had gone terribly wrong. Eddie's mates had scattered, seeing Jackie on the doorstep and Eddie squealing and hightailing it home. They had raised the alarm once they got to their parents.

When the police arrived, they found Jackie sitting on his doorstep, rocking back and forth, mewling. Eddie's right eye was on the path in front of him, in a coagulating pool of blood. A multi-coloured plume had been stuck in it.

* * *

It seems like only yesterday, but three decades have passed. Perhaps that's the reason I've come back, I don't know; the legend says the Parrot Man becomes active again, every thirty years or so. I've walked past my old house and now I stand at the end of Hollerton Drive – I swear I can still smell the fear in the air. It's well-lit now, no more council cutbacks, and it's quiet – it's after two in the morning but...

There – at the end of the street, a hundred yards or so away.

There's a figure. Standing in the shadows between street lamps. It's hunched over, skittish, like something on the hunt. I can't make out its hands but I see something glint, just for a split second, in a stab of moonlight. A blade? A claw..?

It's seen me. It's starting to move – stealthily. Towards me. It can't be; I've come back here after all these years, just to become another victim? The sound of a motorbike reverberates from somewhere away in the distance, and suddenly I'm back in my room, watching Eddie zooming off way too fast up our street. Dad had drunk himself into a stupor after the police had been – and an early grave not too long after – and I sat in my room, listening to him snore. My door was ajar. There was no need to barricade it shut any more. I pulled the bundle of dirty clothes from under my bed; they reeked of sweat and Eddie's blood. I burned them in the compost bin at the bottom of the garden. I tossed the broken bottle in too. The jagged edges still held traces of Eddie's blood. Couldn't be too careful.

The figure is halfway down the street. I see now, it's a youth, swaggering and full of threat. Something glints in his hand. Stepping out of the shadows, so he can fully see me, I pull the feathered cloak around me, the broken bottle gripped tightly in my hand. I can see his eyes now, glimmering wetly. Salivating, I run at him.

THE END

CURIOUS CUTHBERT

By Lynne Phillips

They say curiosity killed the cat, but Gargoyle — the Fairy Queen's cat — was quite safe, curled up on her mistress' lap. It was the queen's son, ten-year-old Prince Cuthbert, whose life was in jeopardy. Once again, his inquisitiveness had landed him in trouble. This time, there was the possibility he might not return to tell the tale.

***

It started when Cuthbert decided to wag school and go fishing instead. He wrote a note — saying he was sick — on his mother's notepaper and magicked it to his wizard tutor. That was a big mistake. His handwriting looked nothing like his mother's beautiful script, so his deception was easy to determine. Cuthbert would be in serious trouble the next time he had to face the teacher, but the possible consequences of that dishonesty paled into insignificance compared to what happened to him later that day.

***

The sun was high in the sky and the day was humid and hot before Cuthbert arrived at his favourite fishing spot. He pried the lid off a can of worms. He'd dug the wriggly, squirmy things out of the vegetable patch the night before. They were difficult to put on the hook, but Cuthbert knew no fish in the river would resist the tasty morsel dangling before its eyes. He hoped the huge number of fish he brought home would appease his parents, and therefore his punishment for wagging school would be minor.

After six hours, Cuthbert placed the last of the fat fish onto a stick, swung it over his shoulder, and as the sun raced towards the horizon, he headed for home. Satisfied twenty fish was enough to feed the whole family, Cuthbert was confident his punishment would probably be going to bed without dinner. Little did he know that before nightfall he would be going without supper, not as a punishment for wagging school, but because he didn't know where he was, and wasn't able to get home.

With the sun sinking fast, he increased his pace along

the path beside the river. His foot — clad only in an open sandal — kicked something hard and metallic.

"Ouch, ouch oooh, that hurt," he said, hopping around on the uninjured foot, holding his stubbed toe which throbbed with pain. "Ouch, ouch!"

Hidden in the mud on the riverbank was the object that caused his suffering. He dug it out of the mud and wiped away some of the dirt. It was a lamp; similar to one in his picture book about a boy named Aladdin.

"I wonder if this is magic like Aladdin's lamp," he said, rubbing it on the sleeve of his shirt. "It would be fun to have three wishes."

If Cuthbert expected a genie to appear, he was disappointed, for no puff of smoke nor magic spirit, to grant him his heart's desire, appeared. When he held the lamp up to the fading light, he saw it was made of a dull metal; perhaps bronze. Its curved spout was covered in an intricate geometric pattern. Tiny writing etched around the base of the lamp was unreadable, not so much because it was small, but because it wasn't in any of the several languages Cuthbert could read. He hoped to figure out what the words etched into the lamp said and if they were a clue how to release the genie within. Instead, they swirled around the base, making it even harder for him to decipher.

The sensible thing would have been to drop the lamp

and hurry home to face the wrath of his parents for wagging school, but Cuthbert loved a challenge and by now his curiosity dared him to try harder to understand the words. The longer he looked at them, the more it gave him a strange feeling. His head felt like a hive of bees had taken up residence in his brain. Everything went black. Dropping his fish, but still clutching the lamp, Cuthbert could feel his head spinning and his body whirling through a dark void.

He seemed to fall forever before he landed with a thump on his bottom on a hard surface.

"Ouch!" he said and rubbed the offending part.

His head still whirled as he tried to determine where he was. Everything was so dark he couldn't even see his own hand in front of his face. With eyes closed, he counted to ten. When he opened them, they had adapted to the darkness. A gigantic black, curved stone roof towered above him and appeared to be some sort of cave with dirt walls and a dusty floor. It was dark, gloomy, freezing cold and rather creepy. He shivered, wrapped his arms around his body against the chill, and evoked a magic spell to create some light. With the glow of his magic surrounding him, Cuthbert felt warmer and less scared. His hands still firmly clutched the lamp.

He counted the minutes and hours in his head and

wondered if his parents were worried when he hadn't returned home before dark. His mother would probably evoke a seeking spell which would have discovered the fish abandoned on the riverbank, but apart from his footprints in the mud, Cuthbert didn't think there were any clues to his whereabouts. Not knowing what to expect next, he waited, hoping someone would appear and explain where he was, and how he could get back to the Elfin Kingdom. Two more hours ticked past; it was way past his bedtime. His eyelids became heavy and he yawned. Maintaining just enough magic to keep him warm, he dimmed the light. The cave became a dark space once again, and he fell into a fitful sleep where he dreamed he was lost and couldn't find his way back home

.

***

Cuthbert woke with a start. Small yellow eyes blinking above him, and the flutter of wings accompanied by a multitude of squeaks and chattering, alerted him that he was no longer alone.

"At last, someone who can help," he said, but he was disappointed to see it was only a colony of microbats arriving back from their nightly scavenge. They swooped above his head; some flying so low he could almost touch them if they weren't so swift. Flying to the roof of the cave, they hung upside down, still squabbling and jostling for space until they settled, and a hush fell over the cave as they slept.

The arrival of the microbats meant there must be an opening to the cave somewhere. If he could discover it, maybe he could find his way back home. In the far distance, he saw a pinprick of light. Brushing the dust off his clothes, he started towards it.

"Left, right, left, right, left!" a loud voice startled him as the sound echoed through the cave.

Cuthbert grinned. "Someone is coming. I will find out how to get home."

"Left, right, left, right, left," the voice boomed.

A dozen moles, marching in formation, approached. He'd seen small, brown, furry moles scurrying through the forest near his home before, but these moles carried long, thick sticks over their shoulders and marched like soldiers.

"Left, right, left, right, left. Company, halt!" the mole at the front boomed. He pointed at Cuthbert. "Arrest the culprit!"

There was a scurry of activity as the other moles scampered out of their ranks and surrounded the startled little prince. They poked him with their sticks. He thought all moles looked the same, but up close he noticed they differed as much as the elves and fairies in his parent's kingdom. Some were short and squat, their legs less than a third of their height. Others were taller and thinner and there was one with longer legs, but a thicker body. Regardless of their size and shape, they all had two things in common: small beady black eyes that glared at him and a tendency to poke him randomly with their sticks. His smile turned to a frown as they poked him harder.

"Ouch, that hurts, be careful," Cuthbert complained and tried to push them away. The moles continued to prod him.

"That's not a friendly way to greet visitors," Cuthbert said

The lead mole stepped closer to Cuthbert. "Lad, you are arrested for the theft of the sacred lamp belonging to our king."

It was only then Cuthbert remembered the lamp, which he still clutched in his hand. He thrust it forward.

"No, you've got it wrong. I didn't steal the lamp. I found it beside the river; embedded in the mud. You can have it back. Then if you'd kindly point me in the right direction, I'd like to go home. My parents will be worried."

The mole's tiny, beady eyes peered at Cuthbert, seeking the lie.

"A likely story when you are so tightly clutching the lamp, but we'll take it and you can argue your case at your trial." He snatched the lamp out of Cuthbert's hands. "There are severe penalties for stealing, especially from the king. Now let's go. Left right, left, right, left, get in step, lad."

The word trial caused Cuthbert's heart to race. He didn't like the sound of that, but he fell in step with the moles, hoping he would have an opportunity to explain his predicament when they reached their destination.

He expected them to head towards the light, but the group wheeled around and headed deeper into the cave. As they marched through a labyrinth of passageways, it became so dark Cuthbert couldn't see where they were going. He guessed the moles knew exactly where they were headed and could see very well in the darkness. When he stumbled, the prod of a stick or two forced him to keep moving.

The group rounded a corner and marched along a shaft with a lower ceiling. Cuthbert realised his eyes seemed to have adjusted to the darkness, or they were approaching an area which was lighter; he wasn't certain which.

After two more right turns, the group marched into a cavernous, well-lit area. Cuthbert grinned at the sight. Hundreds of glowworms randomly blinked on and off;

making the walls sparkle.

The group marched into the middle of the space before the leading mole called, "Company, halt!"

They stopped and waited. Cuthbert was sure what to expect next. The moles surrounding him occasionally poked him with their stout sticks. He was fascinated by the glowworms and would have enjoyed them more if he wasn't so worried about facing a trial for something he didn't do.

BOOM-BOOM-BOOM! The beat of a drum filled the space. The glowworms flicked off their tails, and the area plunged into darkness. For the first time, Cuthbert felt completely lost and afraid. After the pleasure of the glow-worms, the darkness seemed more oppressive and ominous. His legs shook and his heart pounded. He tried to magic some light but failed to raise a spark. He crouched down, hoping to escape, but with their superior eyesight, the guarding moles saw him and prodded him to stand. And there they stood in the oppressive dark, for what seemed an eternity, but Cuthbert was beginning to realise time seemed to be longer in the dark. He knew that was a silly notion, but nothing since he kicked his toe on the lamp made sense.

BOOM, BOOM, BOOM! The drums were getting louder as they approached.

Then silence. Cuthbert's knees knocked and he

shivered as he waited. To his delight, once the drum beat stopped, not only did the glowworms reappear, but thousands of tiny fireflies flew into the dark space, transforming the scary cavernous area into a beautiful fairyland of sparkling lights.

With the fireflies came a horde of moles. Like the soldier moles, they were all sizes and shapes; whole families, with little ones clinging to their backs or scampering along beside the adults. They thronged in filling the once-empty cavern; jostling for a space. There was an air of excitement as their chatter ebbed and flowed until a trumpet sounded. The crowd became silent as a golden coach pulled by six long-legged moles entered. Some moles in the crowd fell to their knees, others bowed low, but they all chanted, "Hail King Humperdink"

Cuthbert was prepared to see a mole wearing a crown and royal robes alight from the carriage, but he was surprised when the mole that emerged was twice as tall as any of the other moles, and instead of being brown, he was an albino. White fur covered his body; his eyes and ears were small and pink. Thick spectacles perched on the end of his rosy snout. He blinked against the glare of the fireflies and raised his paw, shielding his eyes. Instantly, the insects dimmed their lights; still illuminating the space, but replacing the brightness with a soft yellow glow. The glowworms too dulled their tails, until the walls shimmered with tiny pinpricks of light.

The golden carriage left the area and King Humperdink walked to a raised platform Cuthbert hadn't noticed in the dark before.

"Fellow moles, welcome to the annual mole roundup. It is important we gather every autumn to register new births and celebrate the lives of those who are no longer with us. I will hear complaints and settle disputes this afternoon. My courtiers will be available to bring the records up to date. Tonight, we will celebrate the joy of being a mole with a dance and a banquet here in the grand cavern." King Humperdink smiled and the throng of moles cheered. The sound was so loud Cuthbert had to cover his ears.

The albino king raised both paws, and the crowd quietened.

"However, we have more serious business to attend to first. You will all be aware the royal lamp, which has been passed down through the ages, was stolen a week ago. I am pleased to inform you, that not only has it been found, but the thief has been apprehended by our wonderful guards, and he now stands trial. Bring forth the prisoner."

Cuthbert was so engrossed in watching the spectacle,

that he forgot the king was referring to him until the guard moles poked him hard with their sticks and he was forced forward. The crowd booed and jeered.

The king peered at Cuthbert through his thick spectacles.

"Lad, you were found with the lamp in your possession. Your punishment will be five years of hard labour digging new tunnels. Take him away!"

Cuthbert was a prince and not used to being treated so unfairly. He was also cold, hungry, and missing his family, so without thinking, he shouted.

"Now, wait a minute, that isn't fair."

The crowd gasped; no one had ever spoken back to their king before.

Cuthbert stamped his foot. "I demand a fair trial and a chance to prove my innocence. I didn't steal your lamp. It was buried in the mud beside the river where I kicked it with my toe. I'm uncertain how it got to be in the Elfin Kingdom. Perhaps that's what you should be more concerned about. If the lamp is so precious, why didn't you protect it better?"

That caused a murmur to run through the crowd.

The mole king glared at Cuthbert.

"How do you propose to prove you are innocent?" he asked.

Cuthbert remembered a spell his grandfather taught

him that might get him out of this predicament if he could remember the correct sequence of words. It was worth a try.

"Bring me the lamp, and I'll prove not only my innocence but might also show you how your lamp came to be in the mud."

King Humperdink pushed his spectacles back up his nose, leaned forward and said, "I will give you one chance to state your case, otherwise you start digging this afternoon."

Cuthbert stood up tall so he was eye-to-eye with the king. "My grandfather taught me that objects retain memory and, with the correct spell, memories can be revealed."

The crowd of moles booed and hissed. The mass of furry bodies moved closer, but the king nodded and one of the courtiers handed Cuthbert the lamp. Cuthbert felt a faint buzzing in his brain but suppressed it. He didn't want to spin into a black void like last time. With fingers crossed, he muttered his grandfather's spell. A hologram appeared above his head. It showed him walking beside the river carrying the pole of fish over his shoulder, as the sun sank towards the horizon. A titter of mirth came from the crowd of moles when the hapless lad kicked his toe on the lamp and hopped around, holding his stubbed toe and howling. Even the king grinned.

"See. I've been telling you the truth," Cuthbert said.

The mole king nodded. "It seems you are telling the truth. Can you go back further and find out how the lamp came to be in the mud?"

"I'm not sure, but I'll try."

Once again, the elfin prince muttered his grandfather's spell. A large black and tan dog with a white chest and white on his snout trotted along the path; the lamp clearly grasped in his mouth. He stopped, dug a hole, dropped the lamp into it, and scraped the dirt back over.

"Loki!" Cuthbert said. "That makes sense." His father's favourite dog did have a tendency to snaffle things and bury them for later.

"I saw that dog in the tunnels last week," a small mole called out. "He was burying a bone."

"It's only a bit of mischief. Loki doesn't mean any harm. He likes to bury things. He probably thought his bone was a good swap. I'm sorry Loki took your lamp, but it's back now, so if you would be kind enough to point the way back to my home, I would be very grateful. My parents will be worried."

Cuthbert extended his hand to give the king his lamp, but something nagged in his brain and his natural curiosity made him ask, "I'm intrigued by the writing on the base of the lamp. It's not in any of the languages I've been taught. Could you tell me what it says?'

A pinkish tinge appeared on the albino king's face.

"That is secret mole business. You don't need to know our confidence." His face went a deeper shade of pink.

"You don't know, do you!" blurted Cuthbert. "Where did it come from?"

By now, the formerly white-faced mole was a shade of puce. His eyes darted to the courtiers standing beside him as if hoping they had the answers to the questions this irritating lad was asking, but they either hung their heads or looked away, avoiding the king's gaze. He sighed and said, "Many years ago, my ancestors found the lamp when digging a tunnel. All attempts to decipher the words have failed. You are correct. We know nothing about the lamp."

"So, you don't even know if it is a magical lamp?"

The mole king glared at Cuthbert. "Lad, you ask too many questions and you are extremely annoying."

"Wouldn't you like to know more about your lamp?"

"Of course, but we've tried everything."

One of the king's courtiers leaned over and whispered something in the king's ear. The king smiled. He adjusted his crown and leaned towards Cuthbert.

"Instead of so many questions, why don't you

consider if you have some magic which will unlock the lamp's secrets?"

Now it was Cuthbert's turn to blush. Even though he was only ten, he was an elfin prince and had been studying magic for the last five years. He should have thought of casting a spell earlier.

"I'll try, but I can't promise it will work."

"Allakazam, allakazee, lamp, reveal all your secrets to me."

The words swirled around the base, fast to begin with, but they slowed and the letters formed into a language Cuthbert could understand.

He read out loud. "To unlock this lamp's secrets, rub twice in a clockwise direction."

Without waiting for the king's approval, Cuthbert rubbed the lamp, but only a tiny whiff of smoke drifted out of the spout. The mole crowd booed and hissed and the king scowled at him.

"Wait!" Cuthbert yelled above the din as more words appeared. "And once in an anticlockwise direction." He quickly rubbed the lamp. The crowd cheered when a genie emerged.

"Your wish is my command," the genie — who to Cuthbert's delight, looked exactly like the one in his book — said as he floated above the lamp.

Of course, Cuthbert was curious about the genie and

would have liked to stay, but he'd been missing for so long that he knew his parents would be worried. He handed the lamp to King Humperdink.

"The lamp belongs to you to wish for whatever moles desire, but I have one wish, and that is to get back safely to my family."

The king nodded, and the genie clicked his fingers.

***

The sun hung just above the horizon when Cuthbert landed unceremoniously with a thump on his bottom beside the river. The pole — with his fish still fresh — lay where he had dropped it. His forehead furrowed, and he scratched his head in puzzlement before he shrugged, picked up the pole, and continued home to face his punishment for wagging school.

The end

HORROR HIGH SCHOOL FOREVER

By Destiny Eve Pifer

The decaying old school sat among the fallen limbs and dying weeds. Long forgotten, its windows had been broken and its brick façade was covered with graffiti. For years it had been the subject of whispers and gossip. No one could forget the horror that happened within those walls. Three adults and seven students were brutally murdered. The killer was dead and the last remaining survivor who had managed to escape was sitting in a sanatorium.

Now, ten years later five students walked across the broken pavement. They made their way through a hole in a rusty old fence and then jogged toward the boiler room entrance. Only one lagged behind and that was Sarah. The new girl in town Sarah longed to fit in and most of all she longed to get close to her crush Nathaniel. He was the only reason that she came despite having a horrible feeling that something terrible was going to happen. She knew it the night before and now as she was standing there looking up at the old school she felt it even more. The other members of their gang were Paige, Crew, and Tasha. All three were excited about breaking into an old school.

Sarah shivered as she neared and as she stared up at the window she thought she caught a glimpse of someone looking back at her. As they entered the boiler room she reached for Nathaniel's waiting hand. Suddenly Crew lit up a couple of flares and they were able to see their way to the very sight where it all began. Painted in red was a circle with an upside-down pentagram.

"This is it!" said Crew excitedly.

Sarah couldn't believe he was thrilled to be standing in the middle of something that represented evil.

"This is where it all began," said Paige.

"Where what began?" Sarah asked, knowing deep down what the answer was.

"Years ago four students came down here and decided to try a ritual. However, something went horribly wrong and they unleashed something," Nathaniel replied. Sarah could feel her legs beginning to shake.

"It was a demon," Tasha whispered in her ear. She then walked over and draped her arms around Nathaniel's neck.

"Yep they unleashed a demon that went on to possess one of the students who then went on a killing spree," said Crew. Sarah watched as he lit up a cigarette.

"So why are we here?" she asked. All four looked at her.

"Because you are going to use whatever sixth sense you have to tell us exactly what happened that day," Paige replied.

Sarah stepped back with her back against the wall. Not exactly the best defence. If she were smart she would have run but something held her there. "How did they know about her sixth sense?" Then she looked at Nathaniel. She had made the mistake of confiding in him that sometimes she knew what was going to happen before it did. She had been born with the gift but was forced to suppress it until now. Now four of her fellow students expected her to use that gift to see something terrible.

Before she knew it, she was being coaxed into standing in the middle of the pentagram. It was a move that made her uneasy. She stepped into the middle of the pentagram and began to concentrate. Suddenly her mind went blank and she found herself staring at unfamiliar faces.

There were seven of them and she didn't recognize

any of them. It was then that she realized that she had stepped back in the past. She watched as the kids bickered and as they did she smelt a foul stench of sulphur. Something else was in that room, something that wasn't human. An invisible force that seemed to circle around the group of kids before deciding on which one would be its vessel.

Once it did, the light bulbs exploded and the kids ran for the stairs. However, only one remained and it was a handsome boy with a sinister expression on his face. As the other kids tried prying the door open she watched as the possessed boy picked up a heavy wrench and hit one of the other boys in the head. As blood splattered across the faces of the others, she found herself wanting to scream right along with them. Another boy began fighting the possessed one as the janitor opened the door. As the other kids ran screaming down the hall the janitor tried to stop the fight. However, the possessed boy threw him over the edge of the platform and all Sarah could do was watch in horror. The janitor's body lay not far from the other boy. When she looked up she saw the possessed boy looking down at her before walking through the door. She tried to leave the circle but couldn't. It was as though there was a forcefield around it. As blood-curdling screams echoed through the hallway everything went black.

When Sarah awoke, she was back in her own time. The other kids were anxious to hear about what she saw. After she told them, they quickly fled up the boiler room steps. The only one who stayed behind was Nathaniel who helped her up. As they walked up the steps and into the darkness Sarah couldn't help but feel a chill. There were still blood stains in the hallway and with every step, she couldn't help but want to flee. She listened as the others snapped pictures of the horror sites and wondered how they could want to do such a thing. Suddenly there was a heavy breeze that came out of nowhere. As locker doors began to open and shut Sarah found herself reaching for Nathaniel only to find that he wasn't there. Instead, she was standing alone in a dark hallway and at the end, a dark figure stood. She couldn't make out who it was and by the time she got her flash light to turn on the figure was gone. As she walked down the hallway there was an eerie silence.

She never heard the screams. Never heard the figure slash each one of her friend's throats. She never heard a thing until the lights began to flicker on. How odd that there will still be electricity.

Maybe she was losing her mind or maybe just maybe she was waking up. She looked down the hallway and saw the bodies of her friends lying in a puddle of their own blood. Sarah immediately ran towards her and as she did the culprit stepped out from behind

one of the doors. It was Nathaniel except he was covered in blood. He was grinning ear to ear

as he walked towards her. Somehow the demon had survived or maybe it had latched onto her as she travelled through time. Whatever the case, she knew that she wouldn't be able to outrun Nathaniel. He was number one on the track team and she was asthmatic. With no other choice, she made the only sacrifice she could.

"Take me," she said to the demon.

Then, she walked toward Nathaniel and kissed him. The last thing Sarah remembered was walking down the middle of the road. Her body was covered in blood and a strange voice whispering in her head.

The police immediately picked her up and placed her in the same sanatorium as the last remaining survivor of the previous massacre. But this time he wouldn't survive. The demon inside of Sarah would make sure of that. Sarah tried to battle the demon for her soul but in the end, she lost.

THE END

Meet the Authors

John Clewarth was born in the Yorkshire mining village of Featherstone and now lives near the ancient and haunted town of Pontefract where he writes mainly after dark! He has had several of his short stories published or accepted in other anthologies by House of Loki, where his work can be found amongst the stories of many brilliant writers.

As well as being a writer, John was also a teacher for many years. The children he taught were excellent sources of inspiration! He is a natural story-teller and greatly enjoys shaping ideas into tales and fully-developed novels.

His first novel, 'Firestorm Rising', is a spooky tale, inspired by a visit to a gothic graveyard one dark, rainy day. It is aimed at the 8 to 12 age range. His second novel, 'Demons in the Dark', is aimed at the 10-14 age range. John has also written a sequel to Firestorm Rising, The Teardrop of Ice, and has a collection of short stories for all ages, 'Nightmares from the Graveyard', available as an e-book from Amazon or Smashwords.

His latest middle-grade thriller, Jack Devlin and The

Roman Curse, was released in June 2023, by Red Cape Publishing.

John can be contacted on X/Twitter (@johnclewarth), or via his Facebook page (John Clewarth – Author), and his website, (www.johnclewarthauthor.com) for updates on future projects.

Lynne Phillips lives in the Northern Rivers region of New South Wales, Australia. She loves the world of make-believe and magic. With hundreds of stories published in anthologies and online magazines, across most genres, and a second prize in a competition she has found her niche writing for children and young adults. Her passions are reading, writing and keeping fit and her priority is family. She hopes to leave a legacy of well written stories for her grandchildren to enjoy. Connect with her on https://www.facebook.com/lynnephillips.505

Trent Redfield comes from a family of avid readers and has been a lover of the written word since he was young. He has been entranced by fantastical worlds since a librarian placed a copy of The Hobbit in his hands when he was five years old. Over the years, Trent has had poetry, magazine articles, newspaper articles, and essays in several publications. He hopes to build upon his stories and create his own fantastic world to share with others. Encouragement to explore fantasy, mythology, and literature from family, friends, librarians, and teachers is why he is a writer today. Trent has worked as a park guide, park ranger, museum educator, zoo educator, and librarian. He is currently the executive director of a history museum outside Yellowstone National Park.

Gary Rubidge resides in Western Australia, an empty nester with his wife. After his body succumbed to the rigors of competitive sport, he was encouraged to put his story ideas to paper. He relented, took the plunge and is thrilled to have been published at all, let alone in several Drabble anthologies, short stories, a couple of House Of Loki Kids stories, a Tic Toc anthology and as a co-author in the book called 'Disturbed'. There are more story ideas begging to be committed to print when he can find the time to write them. As his wife says – 'He is trying…very trying!'

Facebook: https://www.facebook.com/gary.rubidge.7

Lady Lyndsey Holloway hails from the magical town of Knaresborough (we have our very own Witch!), UK, where she spends most of her time with her head in the clouds, riding on the backs of Dragons. A Scottish Landowner (all 5sqft of it), she is determined to make friends with the faeries and pixies that call the forests their home. Lyndsey lives her life dreaming of magic and mystery. Passionate about reading and writing stories, she spends her time with her husband and two dogs (plus the semi-adopted cat next door), her friends (both real and imaginary), and hopes to have her own Dragon one day. You can follow Lady Lyndsey here:

https://www.facebook.com/groups/199284024728104
https://x.com/LEllisHolloway
https://www.instagram.com/lyndseyellishollowayauthor
https://www.amazon.com/stores/Lyndsey-Ellis-Holloway/author/B07WRPCV9J

Karen B. Jones, a retired Fire Chief and now a fantasy writer, lives in the majestic woods of NW Montana, USA. Her rampant imagination provides endless inspiration.

Lisa H. Owens, a former monthly humorist columnist, resides in North Texas with Fred and Buddy, two elderly rescue dogs, and a wild possum named Harry who lives beneath her backyard shed. Her first published story was a horror memoir about the time she was nearly abducted by Ted Bundy in 1978 at the Royal House Motel in Pensacola, Florida. Her family is often mortified to find Easter eggs hidden within her tales, typically in the form of family secrets and nicknames or private jokes. Read more of her work at www.lisahowens.com.

Jonathan J Bowerman is an author, firefighter, and mentor. He has released his first published book The Secret Realms of the Hidden Elves: The Beginning, in2016. The Beginning is book one of a four-book series. He loves to support fellow authors and provide book reviews and hopes to have a long road of writing and inspiring ahead of him.

Jonathan graduated from Liberty University in 2013 with a Bachelor of Science in Psychology – Christian Counseling with a minor in Global Studies. He believes the time he spent studying, learning, and wrapping his heart and focus around helping others prepared him for the rest of his life. Even though fairly new to the game,

Jonathan enjoys speaking at events, schools, libraries, and anywhere else he can make a difference and spread his passion of writing. Ultimately, his desire is to be an influence on children and young adults everywhere.

Emil Haskett is a Swedish writer of fantasy, horror and science fiction. He has written a novel in Swedish but is mainly a short story writer. His inspiration comes from cold and dark Scandinavian nature. If you just listen to the whispers from woods and lakes the stories will come to you.

Tom Folske lives in Minnesota with his wife, five kids, and three black cats. He has had over 60 short stories published or in the process of being published, with new stories to be featured in upcoming anthologies by British Fantasy Society, Dark Moon Rising Publications, Little Red Bird Publishing, and the Redacted Tales Podcast.

Dawn DeBraal is an internationally known author, living in rural Wisconsin. She has published over 700 short stories, drabbles, and poems in online ezines and anthologies. She was a 2019 Pushcart nominee, awarded the international Literary Global Book Award for her first solo novel 2024 "The Lord's Prayer, A Series of Horror," 2024 Weird Wide Web short story contest winner, and Runner up in Endless Ink short story horror contest 2023. She tends to lean toward the horror genre because it makes her life seem so much better. Dawn also writes under the penname of Garrison McKnight.

https://www.facebook.com/All-The-Clever-Names-Were-Taken-114783950248991

https://linktr.ee/dawndebraal

https://www.amazon.com/stores/author/B07STL8DLX/allbooks

Hailing from the east coast of Canada, Brian MacGowan is currently madly typing away in Indiana, U.S.A. where he lives with his wife and two daughters. His short stories have been published in a variety of anthologies. Brian enjoys confusing his coworkers with the Canadian spelling and pronunciation of many words. He receives particular enjoyment when he gets to verbally spell any word that contains a zed. In between writing short stories, Brian is working on a paranormal novel based in part on an actual haunted opera house.

In Memory Of Our Dear Friend
Nicholas Wilkinson

Find out more about Nick and check out the amazing stories he wrote for young people and adults here:
House-of-loki.com/our_nick

Read the first chapter for free or buy a copy at
greenspike-art.com

House-of-loki.com/books

www.ingramcontent.com/pod-product-compliance
Lightning Source LLC
LaVergne TN
LVHW010317070526
838199LV00065B/5589